Seven Daughters

ALSO BY JESSICA LOUREY

FICTION
The Catalain Book of Secrets (2015)
Seven Daughters: A Catalain Book of Secrets novella (2015)

MYSTERIES
May Day (2006)
June Bug (2007)
Knee High by the Fourth of July (2007)
August Moon (2008)
September Fair (2009)
October Fest (2011)
November Hunt (2012)
December Dread (2012)
January Thaw (2014)
February Fever (2015)

FANTASY
The Underrock: A Savage Sagas novella (2014)

YOUNG ADULT
The Toadhouse Trilogy: Book One (2012)

Seven Daughters

JESSICA LOUREY

Seven Daughters: A Catalain Book of Secrets Novella
ISBN-13: 978-0-9908342-8-1

Cover designed by Scarlett Rugers Design, www.scarlettrugers.com.

The Catalain family tree as well as the pages from the actual Catalain *Book of Secrets* were designed by Tony Van Den Einde.

TOADHOUSE
BOOKS

DEDICATION

To Linda Joffe Hull, a fantastic writer, editor, and friend.

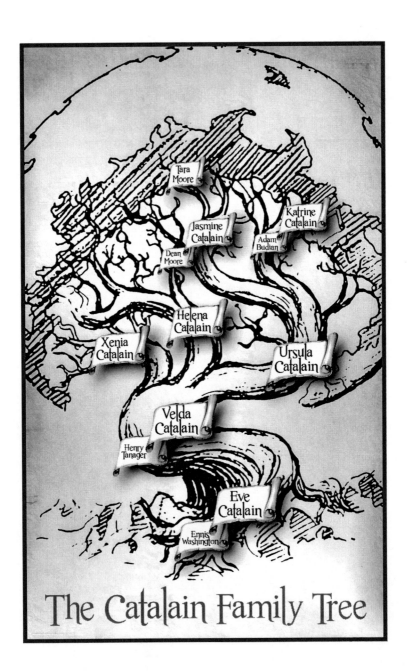

The Catalain Family Tree

PROLOGUE

Land speculator James A. Faith, originally from Chicago, staked a townsite claim on a riverbank in what is now northwest Minnesota in 1882. Rivers were the heartblood of transportation and industry back then, and the Ojibwe people outnumbered whites five to one. The native people called the river Ahmiknibi, or beaver water, for all the dam-building creatures populating the shores. Faith called the rust-colored waterway Rum River. He made his claim on a wide flat spot next to a bend, and then packed up his pick and gold pan, intending to head west.

Three hundred yards from his claim, he encountered a group of Indians who, through a series of unintelligible (to James) words and increasingly frustrated hand gestures, led him two more miles upstream to the most beautiful waterfalls he'd ever laid eyes on. He had never been much for poetry, but if he'd been born in a different time and better-looking, he might have waxed on about how the air around the falls smelled of freedom and the water spray caught the sunlight like the jeweled crown of Mother Nature herself. But, since no man can escape his upbringing, he instead grunted, thanked the Indians for showing him where the best part of the river was located, and began to build a meager fence, enough to demonstrate that he'd improved the land.

The Indians grew increasingly agitated the more he built, their hands flying with an effort to get him to understand. Things may have ended differently if James A. Faith spoke Ojibwe, but he'd found English and a Sharps self-cocking Model 1851 were all the communication skills he needed. So when the Indians made the wavy signs in the air and talked about *ginebegoogs,* he listened exactly as well as he had when they pointed at the river and made biting motions and muttered "*Ahmiknibi.*"

In other words, he didn't listen at all.

"Well, thank you kindly," he'd said, when he grew weary of their pantomime. He strung the last bit of barbed wire to a tilting fencepost, tossed them each a silver coin for their trouble, jumped atop his horse—a precarious proposition given his girth—and rode west, planning a brief detour to Fort Snelling to file his Minnesota Territory claim.

The Ojibwe watched him ride away, shaking their heads. When they'd steered him upstream, it hadn't been to show him the beautiful falls. It had been to point out the *ginebegoog* that were about to surface all along the river.

Turns out, spurred by an internal clock only they could read, tens of thousands of snakes in this exact spot would unravel from a great, underground writhing ball and slither topside, devouring every small creature that crossed their paths. In fact, the earth was already rumbling with their birth. James A. Faith would have spotted the first of their heads poking through the spongy ground of the riverbank and heard the beginning of their susurrus song if he'd bothered to glance behind him when riding off. This section of the river was a powerful place, and also a very bad location for building.

The Ojibwe shrugged. They'd tried to warn him.

After filing his claim, Faith rode as far as the Black Hills in the Dakota Territory, where he caught the front end of the gold rush and made a name for himself as a loud, red-faced drinker with a lucky nose for land. He fell in love with an Oglala woman named Lootah Maka who he met while hunting bear in the Black Hills, and he was true to her—a first for him, despite his name—until he drew his last breath.

He liked his Black Hills fame and never returned to the town he'd named after himself or the landmark where he'd staked his claim. He carried a fondness in his heart for Faith Falls as it was the first land he'd ever titled, but he believed it was too far off the beaten track to amount to much. He died in 1897 in his yellowed underwear, his throat slit by a stranger he'd cheated in poker the night before, never having returned to Minnesota.

"I ever tell you all that before?" Albrikt Gottfridsen asked, pausing in his story. "About him dying in his underwear?" He and Philander Willmar rocked in separate chairs on Albrikt's front porch on River Street. Both men puffed on fresh-dried tobacco in their corncob pipes. It was April of 1907. "An Ojibwe used to come by the store regularly told me the whole tale. I imagine the Indian embellished a bit, but what's a good story otherwise?"

Philander rocked silently.

Philander and Albrikt had been the first white settlers in Faith Falls, arriving two years after Faith staked his claim. They'd witnessed rutted paths evolve into dusty roads and hewn-log cabins become storefronts, the latter crafted of fresh-sawn hardwoods purchased from Albrikt's upstream mill.

Faith Falls had become a hub in the northwestern section of the state. Farmers and foresters brought their goods into town for trade, and their business supported saloons, restaurants, and hotels, along with doctors, dentists, and assorted paper collars. The population grew enough to support two churches, one Lutheran and one Catholic, each assuring the other that there was plenty room for both with a smile and a curse.

"I said, Philander, have I told you the story of the founding of Faith Falls before, and of Faith's old underwear? I'm sure I have. The part about the snakes is certainly pure bull, but I enjoy the detail of the yellowed underwear." He chuckled and scratched at a mosquito bite on his arm. Albrikt and Philander were white-haired by now, having front-row seats to the birth and growth of their town.

"Suppose it's the full moon making the ground rumbly and the people so sulky?" Albrikt asked, switching subjects. The ground in and around Faith Falls had been echoing for a week, sparking talk of earthquakes in Minnesota. People had been short with one another, riled up by the early and warm spring, similar to the one that had occurred the year James A. Faith staked his claim, if Philander had bothered to add the facts up. An accidental bump in the street was likely to turn into a fistfight, and honest children were driven to steal sweets and marbles for reasons they could not explain.

Albrikt took short puffs deliberately out of sync with his rocking, the missing joint of his pinky finger—a trait he would pass on to 80% of his descendants, along with hair the color of copper—outlined by the pipe. "Because," he continued, 25-year's accustomed to Philander's quiescence, "If Emma breaks one more dish and then hollers at me for it, I'm going to have to start increasing her sleeping draught."

Philander rocked some more.

"With this warm spring, there's worries about the mouse plague coming. Did you hear that, Philander?"

Philander finally nodded, his white hair unmoved by the breeze. He had been an apothecary his entire working life, and a small-town one at that. Talk of plagues perked him up like nothing else could, at least for a short while.

"The *Daily Republican* reports Fargo being overrun," Albrikt continued. "The mouse plague started out West with this unnatural warm spring, and it's moving east right along with it. The postman has family in Fargo, and he says the rodent noise is enough to make an honest man drink. Always chittering and scurrying. Millions of mice, he says. They run up your legs, steal your hair for nests while you sleep, and poison any animal that eats 'em. The whole town reeks of mouse piss, and there's hardly any food left. You can't even tie up a side of salt pork because the mice'll climb any wall to get at it."

Philander had dozed off in the middle of Albrikt's musings, his smoking pipe clutched close to his chest, so he missed the first breeding ball of garters choosing that exact moment to roll past like a toy escaped from the underworld. Albrikt spotted it, though, and choked in mid-sentence. His pipe dropped from his mouth with a clatter, red embers scattering in the warm April breeze.

"What in the Sam Hill…"

A scream soon followed as more mating balls rolled down Main Street. Those garters not lucky enough to join a group slithered solo until the streets ran like mercury with snakes. It was exactly as the Ojibwe who'd told Philander the story of James A. Faith had predicted, if Albrikt had bothered to listen on a deep level, one that required commitment. As it was, Albrikt could only mutter a begrudging, "I'll be *goddamned*. That old Indian was telling the truth."

The invasion lasted three days, during which people dared not step outside if they didn't have to. That didn't stop the snakes from entering buildings through cracks in the floors to nestle in empty boots or curl next to sleeping babies, as the nights were still chilly despite the unseasonable heat.

The light scraping sound of their bodies was repulsive, the sheer numbers and the sight of crawling, writhing serpents even worse, but it was the smell that was unbearable, like a jar of urine and sweat left in the sun too long. Some in town wanted to write to the state government for help, but they were too afraid to leave their homes for the post office.

For all the horror, the snakes also brought providence. A boy climbing to escape the snakes found a lucky quarter he'd hidden from his sister and forgotten about. An alto in the church choir bolted into the Faith Falls Saloon to escape the squirming serpents and collided with the preacher she would later marry, he with no intention of stopping in the sleepy town until the snakes made it impossible to simply pass through. Albrikt's own wife ran to escape the snakes, fell, and broke her clavicle. If not for the subsequent chest x-ray, her tuberculosis would have likely gone undiscovered until it was too late.

And, as suddenly as they arrived, the snakes disappeared.

Some claimed the unholy creatures slid west to feast on mice, and indeed, newspaper records reveal the Fargo Mouse Plague ended shortly thereafter. Other townsfolk crossed themselves and declared that the snakes had returned to hell to gather more numbers. Albrikt, always a sensible man, reassured everyone who entered his sawmill that it was no more than a freak gloaming, though he quietly invested in taller boots.

In the hub-bub of the receding snakes, he and other members of the Faith Falls' Boosters almost missed welcoming a new couple to town: Eva and Ennis Catalain. It was curious to Albrikt that the reptiles had arrived around the same time as the Catalains, and that the two comings seemed tied together, somehow. It wasn't because the snakes and the new couple were alike in their appearance, though there was something animal in the way Eva's green eyes flashed with secret knowledge and how Ennis always seemed to be measuring people, despite his hearty handshake and open smile. Nor was there any similarity between the townspeople's reactions to the reptiles or their feelings toward the husband and wife. The snakes woke a primal fear, whereas the Catalains were loved, at least at first. It wasn't even the coincidental timing of their arrivals because the memory of the snakes vanished like molt, but once you met Eva and Ennis, you could never forget them.

Maybe it was because like the snakes, the Catalains brought magic to Faith Falls.

Where exactly they had come from had never been clear. Some said New Orleans, some said Boston, but whatever the specific city, everyone knew they came from money. After she and Ennis built their gorgeous Queen Anne, Eva threw elaborate parties in her home and organized town dances and the annual mummer's parade. Her homemade spirits were legendary, and a charming rumor began to circulate that her mulled hard cider was so delicious that it could turn back time, though surely only those who drank too much believed it. She welcomed enough people from every class into her home that gossip against her was impossible to sustain, though some inevitably tried.

Ennis was an impeccable host and active in local government. He and Eva also travelled frequently, bringing back curious and new styles from faraway lands. They were the sparkle in Faith Falls until their house went up for auction during the Great Depression, and they disappeared from the town and the lives of its inhabitants.

At first, the talk was of how dreary the town was without them, and concern for their well-being. Soon, though, the memories of Eva's graciousness and Ennis' cascading belly laugh faded. The stoic Scandinavians instead focused on the Catalains' frivolity, and how they never seemed to work, and how their baby girl Velda was practically raising herself. Within ten years, the name Catalain, when remembered, brought a sneer and a sharp, bile-scented story, one that could make the listener's heart burn. He in turn would grow angry at the Catalains for that pain and pass it down the line.

And like the memory of the snakes, the Catalain's Queen Anne began to fade, and become blurry around its edges.

§

Forty-three years after the Catalains arrived, Faith Falls experienced another unseasonably warm spring and the rumbling of the earth began to attract the attention of the U.S. Geological Survey in Mounds View, Minnesota. By this time, both Philander and Albrikt had passed on, permanently gone from the town they'd built on the back of Faith's claim and a mammoth nest of snakes.

People rejoiced in the sixty-degree weather, women prematurely yanking their pedal pushers and spring dresses out of storage and men driving with their tops down. Ice cracked early on the river, and the water flowed free. The lilacs shivered but were not fooled. This wasn't spring. It was another gloaming.

"Snakes Take Over Faith Falls, Minnesota," read the March of 1965 headlines as far away as San Francisco. The town was overrun, businesses closed, and residents' lives were turned inside out. The snakes continued to pour like a spring-fed river down the streets.

Even more fantastical than the legions of snakes were the stories of miracles accompanying them—a paraplegic in the Avignon neighborhood who could suddenly walk, lovers reunited in the Faith Falls nursing home after 40 years of fruitless searching, a man living in a downtown apartment who thought he heard snakes in the walls and began ripping out the plaster and lathe and instead discovered a fortune in gold. People began to buzz, and the stories of snakes and miracles spread throughout the country.

And quietly, hardly a blip amidst all the publicity and excitement, the husband of Velda Catalain, daughter to Eva and Ennis, was murdered and buried without investigation, though Midge Gottfridsen, granddaughter to Albrikt, noticed, and the injustice burned her deeply. She had loved Henry, after all, though he had never returned her affections beyond a single night stolen from Velda.

Then, two days after the snakes arrived, a farmer in Oklahoma witnessed a flying saucer land on his silo. He claimed it used a mounted ray gun to suck up cows like spaghetti noodles. His picture proof looked suspiciously like a Jiffy Pop container resting astride a painted oatmeal canister. Nevertheless, newspaper reporters covered it voraciously, headlines screaming about an alien attack, and soon, the nation forgot about the snake invasion.

And as before, in Philander's time, the people of Faith Falls forgot as well. But science never forgets. This is why the Country Inn and Suites on Highway 210 is currently booked solid, hosting herpetologists from all over the world who are assembling in Faith Falls to witness and record the emergence of the world's largest redlined garter snake communal ball. The weather pattern is right. The Richter scale has measured the telltale temblors. The snakes are certainly on their way. Again.

This time, they were not only bringing magic, but also a cataclysmic confrontation between the Catalains and the Gottfridsens that's been a long time coming.

Chapter 1

Spring weather came calling the first week in March—prematurely, for Minnesota—a wash of thaw and trembling green. The ground was periodically overtaken by rumbling. The unnaturally warm weather made townspeople so generous that rather than worry about the rumblings underfoot, they decided to name them.

"Did you feel that earth thaw this morning? Knocked a vase clear off my nightstand."

"That was nothing! There was an earth thaw just this afternoon that cracked the ground right in front of me. Almost lost my dog to it!" Laughing and head-shaking would ensue, and they'd move on to talking about the growing season, or the movies, or their children.

The scientists in the Country Inn and Suites already had a name for the rumbling—the snake awakening, or the snakening, if they were among like-minded friends and had swallowed a drink or two—but who worries about scientists when the air smells like fresh-sliced celery and is just as green? Not Helena Catalain.

"Turn your car off."

Helena obeyed without question. It wasn't just the robotic voice. It was also that she was reluctant to be any trouble to anyone, even an automated car wash. Besides, it was a gorgeous spring afternoon, dappled with lemony sunshine, warbling birds, and enough promise to make you kiss a stranger. Why do anything but smile on such a day?

The old yellow van that she shared with her twin sister, Xenia, was yanked forward into the carwash bay. *Good.* She'd been nervous guiding it into the tracks, but she must have placed it right. The bay door closed behind her, and a massive blue brush spun toward the van's hood. The smell of soap and wax filtered into her vehicle, and the first gentle patters of water fell on the roof.

It wasn't until the water spritzed out from the tubes on the wall that Helena realized she hadn't rolled up the front windows.

Either of them.

The first shot of water landed north of her ear, pinning her gray-blonde hair to her skull in a soapy fritz. The second streamed in through the passenger side, soaking a pile of receipts. She couldn't roll up the windows. They were electric, and the robot had been clear that she was to leave her car off.

So, Helena made the best of it.

She moved the wet pile of paper to the backseat, serendipitously ducking the spray launching toward her neck, unbundled the emergency rain jacket stuffed next to the first aid kit, and tugged it on, ignoring the annoying twinge in her left side. Then she settled in.

The spray created a soothing rhythm, an orchestra of water thrumming on the passenger seat, followed by the percussion of the spray to her shoulder or head, ending with a melodic, metallic ripple across the roof of the van. Then, the whole pattern repeated. Her foot tapped to the beat.

The car wash—which had morphed into a "Helena wash"— had been an impulse stop. She'd left Seven Daughters Candy and Clothes shortly after closing to run errands, including stopping by the post office to drop off bills and driving forty miles to Alexandria for the organic turbinado sugar she dusted her maple truffles with.

Xenia and Helena had put a down payment on the building that became Seven Daughters fourteen years earlier. Before that, Helena sold homemade candy out of her older sister Ursula's Queen Anne kitchen and Xenia tailored clothes in a small room off the back that she had converted into a sewing space. They built a burgeoning clientele on word of mouth, and it hadn't taken much convincing for them to make it official once Ursula's girls moved out and Helena and Xenia's childcare services were no longer needed.

Seven Daughters was launched.

The store was small, a renovated restaurant two blocks off River Street in downtown Faith Falls, Minnesota, a sleepy burg with bronze otter statues parading along the main streets and a ring of box stores squeezing the outskirts. Helena hired Artemis X. Buckley, a local carpenter infamous for tying 523 helium balloons to his favorite lawn chair and floating to Pelican Lake, to remodel the restaurant's kitchen. She kept the old-fashioned dessert coolers but had Artemis redo their shelves so she could fill them with tantalizing truffles, her specialty.

Artemis had recently reentered her life. He'd been pleasant enough when he'd remodeled the store's kitchen fourteen years earlier, and Helena had to admit to developing a bit of a crush on him back then. He'd never asked her out, though, and she didn't want to violate the employer-employee relationship, so she hadn't come on to him despite her desire.

In the past year, though, he'd begun spending time with Velda, Helena's mother and daughter to Eva and Ennis, the first Catalains in Faith Falls. Velda had a reputation for being a runabout despite being in her 70s, and Helena assumed the two were dating, though Artemis was at least fifteen years younger than her mother. She was sad that he was off the market, but she'd come to terms with it. Her sisters and mother might not care much for faithfulness, but Helena placed a premium on it, which is why she'd been uncomfortable with his recent visits to Seven Daughters, the most embarrassing occurring just today.

She'd just called Xenia over to the counter to try a new truffle recipe she'd been playing with for weeks. It was a blend of black currant and flax seed rolled in dark chocolate. She'd crafted it in response to a customer who'd complained about hot flashes. The result was a candy with a deep purple center that tasted like succulent fall grapes and church giggles. She was thinking of calling it Believe in Change, but was worried people would think it was a political statement rather than a menopausal one, and she didn't want to upset anyone.

Xenia was popping a truffle into her mouth when Artemis entered the store, his black fedora resting jauntily on his head. Helena immediately dropped below the cooler, still clutching the tray of truffles. "I'm not here," she'd whispered from her crouching position, steadying her breath. She really would have to get better at confrontations. In the meanwhile, hiding worked.

Xenia's eyebrows knit together and her gaze traveled to the front door. "Is it Artemis? Because I don't think he's going to leave without talking with you. This'll be the third time this week he's stopped by, and he's not coming for the dresses."

Helena frowned. Xenia was right, despite the teasing tone of her voice. She'd best deal with this head on. Tell Artemis straightaway that she wasn't interested and didn't appreciate him running around on her mother. Give him a piece of her mind. Let him know—

"Mmmhmm." Xenia's warning cough was polite, but too late. Artemis was peeking over the top of the truffle case that he'd redesigned, peering at the top of Helena's head.

"Hello, Ms. Xenia." Artemis smiled, and his face wrinkled in all the right places. He was a small man, lean as beef jerky, whose name was bigger than he was. He'd respectfully removed his hat. "You too, Ms. Helena. Did you drop something?"

Just my dignity. Helena straightened herself. She faced Artemis, smoothing her dress and intentionally ignoring Xenia's under-her-breath laughter. Helena's intention was to be firm, but when she met his gaze, she had a hard time not smiling back. His face was just so open. She fought the urge, though, and kept her expression and voice steady. "Just loading the case, Mr. Buckley."

His glance dropped. He tapped the glass. "Is that a new candy?"

Xenia nodded and answered before Helena had a chance. "She's calling it 'The Change.'"

Helena didn't correct her sister.

"Could I buy one?"

Helena's eyes widened. She would certainly have to draw the line here. She wasn't sure what the candy would do to a male. Probably nothing, but he wasn't her target audience. "I'm afraid it's still in the testing phase."

But Xenia was too quick for her. She snatched a candy off the wax paper and handed it to Artemis before Helena's sentence had left her lips. Artemis tossed the haystack-shaped truffle into his mouth. She watched him chew. His skin took on a light purple hue for the briefest moment, and his blue eyes shaded violet. Helena had to blink twice to make sure her eyes weren't deceiving her, and by then, the effect had passed.

"Dip me in honey, that was delicious!" Artemis appeared no worse for the wear. If anything, his smile was even wider. "I'll take two more to go."

"How are you feeling?" Helena studied his face intently.

"Like I want to hug the world."

This time, Helena couldn't help herself. She smiled back. A humming spark the color of a blue moon traveled from her smile to Artemis' chest, and his grin turned into full-out laughter. He passed the emotion right back to Helena. It grew. Both of them doubled over in the giggles, for such was the power of Helena's candies.

They were delicate, each no larger than a wild plum, shaped like sea shells, flowers, intricate animals, or arcane symbols, whatever inspired her when she was crafting them. Some of her candies were jewel-colored sugar spun into glass and others were pure dark, sweet, or white chocolate, as creamy as love, but most had fillings—smooth buttercream or crunchy roasted almonds, fluffy ganache or sugared lime, whatever claimed her fancy. She'd even crafted a limited time maple bacon truffle—sweet and salty—after eating a pint of pistachio ice cream right before bed and having the strangest dream about pigs in Vermont.

Regardless of content and appearance, every one of Helena's candies carried magic, though she'd never admit it to anyone but herself. Her Lilac Love chocolates were the most popular, made of a chocolate so dark it melted down your throat like an elixir. Helena shaped the chocolate to resemble the delicate flutes of lilac petals, and injected them with a crystalline sweet center she crafted from distilled spring flowers. One bite of the silken treasure revealed the eater's true love.

Peppermint Secrets were the second-best seller. They were crafted of white chocolate molded into a delicate leaf shape with veins of exquisite green mint laced through. Helena recommended those for people whose stomachs were upset by guilt. The Sweet Dreams truffle was delicious, too, filled with lavender-infused honey and dusted with sugared chamomile. Helena always cautioned people not to operate heavy machinery while eating the Sweet Dreams as it was impossible to finish it without falling asleep.

She demurred when asked for her recipes, made no claims about the properties of the chocolates other than that they would taste delicious. And they did, always, as beautiful to the tongue as they were to the eye. Over the years, she'd gleaned a lot of information from her customers, more than a bartender or even a hairdresser would hear in the course of their day, and she often stayed late to concoct special orders for the woman whose husband was cheating or the teenage boy who wanted a gift for the girl he was too shy to ask out.

When customers weren't sharing their most secret desires with round, happy Helena, they were worshipping the racks of gorgeous dresses in Xenia's section of the store. Though the sisters shared the same till, Helena limited the face of her business to the dessert coolers. Xenia spread her wares over the rest of the main room, setting up her dress racks where diners used to swap farm stories across checkered tablecloths.

She sewed every kind of dress that had ever existed, from simple baby dolls to formal ball gowns, and each one was unequivocally flattering to the woman who bought it. A vacationer who'd wandered into the store by accident the first year Seven Daughters was open discovered that a 50s-style, deep plum A-line dress perfectly balanced her wide hips with her strong shoulders. If you were lucky enough to have your prom dress sewn by Xenia, you were guaranteed a kiss that would return to you on your deathbed like a lace-wrapped gift. Flat-chested? Wearing one of Xenia's flapper dresses awoke you to how amazing your arms were, and what a gift it was to be able to walk through the world in your tight, safe body. Jiggly belly? Xenia's marmalade-orange, accordion-pleated sundress would hang off you beautifully, swirling and dancing in the breeze, reminding you and the world of the stunning, wise beauty in your eyes and heart.

The demand for Xenia's designs expanded to the point where she had to register customers and impose a limit—one dress per person per year. Some maneuvered around it, but on the whole, the ladies in the know were willing to support each other. Xenia sewed all the dresses herself, and Helena baked, stirred, and poured only with family watching. These were habits of efficiency more than a desire to keep their secrets, and in fact, they'd recently been talked into offering sewing and cooking classes through community education. They didn't have the time, but it felt like the right thing to do.

They'd also hired an assistant, though today was his day off, which is why Helena had run the errands on her own after some pleasant small talk with Artemis, whom she would absolutely never date but whose company she was coming to appreciate. She'd finished all her after-work duties and was on her way home when she'd passed the car wash, a sign out front claiming "We get your car cleaner than anyone in town for cheaper! Stop by and let us scrub away any doubts!"

She'd taken them up on their generous offer.

She was humming as the arc of water wound down, offering one final, gentle kiss of liquid on her soaked left scalp. The car wash's exit door yawned open. When directed, she started her van and opened the remaining windows to help dry out the slushy carpet in the front. Then she pointed the vehicle toward home, her hums morphing into words: *days may be cloudy or sunny, we're in or we're out of the money…*

She couldn't place the song, but singing the words made her happy, so she kept it up on the drive, while she parked, and as she sashayed through the Queen Anne's back door.

"What the deuce happened to you?"

The song dropped from Helena's lips. Xenia was staring open-mouthed at her, a steaming pot of noodles in her hands. Helena followed her sister's gaze and realized she was dripping onto the floor. She slipped off the raincoat and hung it on the hook inside the door.

"An unexpected shower." Helena smiled. She loved her twin more than the sun loved the earth. Though the two of them could not be more different in personality or appearance, they'd never been apart for more than a day or two in their 50 years.

Xenia opened her mouth and then closed it, opened it again, and settled for shaking her head. "We're having tofu pad Thai for dinner. Just you and me. Ursula is in the Cities for a few days. Why don't you go clean up first?"

Helena's smile widened. She pecked Xenia's cheek as she walked past her. "How lucky am I? Two showers in one day, and someone to make dinner for me."

She made her way through the Queen Anne's huge kitchen, her favorite room in the house. The Queen Anne had been built in the early 1900s by Helena's grandparents, Eva and Ennis, whom she'd never met. They'd lost the gorgeous home in the Great Depression, and it fell into disrepair. The glorious wraparound porch began to sag, the tiny oriels in the turret were broken accidentally or by vandals and boarded over. The luscious burgundy paint began to peel and the house took on a frowning, haunted countenance. When her older sister Ursula returned to Faith Falls in the 70s, she had enough money—just—to buy and begin remodeling the house back to its former glory. When it was habitable, she'd invited her beloved sisters to live with her, and Xenia and Helena had each taken their own room on the second floor.

Helena made her way up the stairs and into her room, grateful as always for the sturdiness of her door, the strength of the wood under her feet, the safeness and love the house surrounded her with. She closed the door behind her and started to change clothes, wincing as she pulled her shirt over her head. Her left breast hurt, and so did her armpit.

She knew why.

Evening was padding in, and her east-side room was shadowy. The only light spilled in through a restored oriel. The sunlight hit the full-length mirror at a perfect angle, almost like a spotlight. She strolled over, dropping her slacks, shirt, and her underpants as she walked. They hit the ground with a wet plud.

She gazed into the mirror. A fifty year-old woman stared back at her, her eyes tired, her mouth drawn now that there was no one around to smile at. Her body was a soft curving sea of flesh with silvery fish swimming at the edges of her hips, thighs, and breasts. She ran her hands over her chest, and her wide hips that had held lovers in ecstasy, and arms that had carried thousands of pans of sweet and comforting candy to eager mouths, and her belly with its two curves—one for the meal and one for dessert, she liked to think.

She continued, caressing her fabulous rear end, which seemed to grow a little wider every year but never any deeper, and rubbed her powerful thighs as she let her eyes walk down to her knees, which she'd always recognized as beautiful, ending with her little toe, the one that curved under and in. Her magnificent flesh jiggled as she moved, and she caught a glimpse of this in the mirror. It brought her the tiniest smile, so she shook her hips harder, and the surface of her rolled like the ocean. This made her laugh, and so she danced, naked, in the fading spring sunlight.

While she danced, she tried her best not to look at her chest. The breasts were still full despite her age, magnificent, knocking orbs with nipples as large as cracked eggs accenting each in tender pink.

They were perfect but for the puckered, poisonous scaling that circled her left aureola like a storm cloud before disappearing into her armpit.

Her breast was rotting. Seeing it made her stomach twist, every time, so she looked away.

She didn't want to be any trouble to anyone, even herself.

The Catalain Book of Secrets:
Conquering Fear

When it's not in the hands of children or idiots, fear is the most useful tool you're given in this life, right ahead of discomfort. Fear signals where you should go and what you are meant to face, serving as both a sign and a ladder. However, this ladder is easily twisted into a cage if you ignore its summoning. Use this spell when you find yourself imprisoned rather than elevated by your fears.

You'll need either a candle or a plant. Choose based on your affinity to fire or earth. Also gather a square of paper, an ink pen, and enough stones to tightly circle the plant or candle, whichever you've chosen.

1. *Write your fear in a circle in the center of the paper square, avoiding writing in the corners. Be honest and specific.*

2. *Fold the paper four times, until it is a smaller, stiffer square.*

3. *Place it either under the candle or bury it in the dirt of the plant (if it's a big fear, and you don't live in a wintry climate, an outdoor plant or tree works beautifully).*

4. *Circle the candle or the plant with your stones. They are your fortress, your strength, your true knowledge. Say the following as you place each stone: "Fear is my guide, and I am strong."*

5. *If you've chosen the candle, burn it until it puts itself out. If you've chosen the plant, thank it for composting your fear and turning it into something useful.*

6. Do what you will with the stones. The spell is set, and your cage is open.

CHAPTER 2

"I can help sew, you know," he'd said a week after he was hired.

"If you watch the till and keep the racks tidy, that'll be help enough," Xenia had said.

He'd tried Helena next. "My dad says I'm a good cook."

"That's nice," Helena had murmured, focused on adjusting a pile of confectionery rulers. Her double-boiler of dark chocolate was cooling, and she needed to pour it into the paper-dollar-sized rectangles before it became too thick. When it was poured, it would flatten over the almond paste into a thin wafer of bitter sweetness, into which she'd carve a perfect replica of a dollar before sprinkling it with green sugar. Dark, rich chocolate, ideal for those who had money problems.

"I bet I could help you with the candy. You know, be your assistant."

"Oh," Helena said, not glancing up. He stood, hands in pockets, for ten full minutes, watching Helena's every movement with the intensity of a supplicant. When a tinkling bell announced new customers, he'd returned to the front. He was good at his job, unobtrusive, helpful, smart. That had been last summer, the season before his senior year, and he'd only gotten better since. Helena didn't know what they'd do without him when he graduated come June.

But that was the future. The now was a humming Thursday. A busload of tourists on their way to the casino on the other end of the county had stopped in downtown Faith Falls, and a clot of them had entered the store, whispering about the cost of the beautiful chocolates.

"Each one is handmade," Helena heard Leo say. "We don't use artificial ingredients. There's no wax in the chocolate."

The tourists flashed tight smiles, but if they didn't taste a chocolate or try on a dress, they didn't know what they were missing. It was just food and clothing, and they were saving their money for slots. Leo didn't pressure them. Xenia had scolded him the one time she'd caught him doing the hard sell.

"This isn't a time share."

"But everyone loves your dresses when they try them on," he'd said.

"Some things you need to arrive at on your own. We've got plenty of customers as it is."

Leo hadn't sulked. He'd processed her words and changed his behavior. He was that observant, and he'd never tried to twist anyone's arm since. He simply told them what they were looking at and left the rest up to them.

"Do you have very much homework?" Helena asked Leo, closing the door of the display case. She asked him this every school night he worked for them. Every time, the answer was the same, or close to it.

"Naw. Got it done during study hall."

"Good." Helena was never sure if she believed him. She suspected he was the type of boy who could be lazy and still earn good grades. He was a kind soul, too, almost too tender for this world. Leo had confessed to her that since his mother had died two years earlier, he'd tried living down in the day-to-day world, but the hot exhaust of humanity made him sleepy. Seven Daughters was the one place he could breathe. "I'm glad to hear that about your schoolwork. Because—"

She stopped in midsentence, her heart pounding.

Meredith Baum née Gottfridsen had just strode into the store.

She was a woman with breath like a two-stroke engine and eyebrows that appeared as though they'd been pasted on backward. One glance at her, and you knew she had been a sour baby. Though she'd taken on her husband's name when they'd married thirty years earlier, she was a Gottfridsen to her core, from her crown of copper hair to her stubby pinkies, and she'd snatched up the family mantle with zest if not grace. Specifically, she'd taken it as her guiding purpose in life to undo the Catalains.

Her great-grandfather, Albrikt Gottfridsen, had been enamored of the Catalains when Eva and Ennis initially moved to Faith Falls. He hadn't lived to see the town's devotion die. When the railroad came through in 1932, Albrikt was ten-year's dead and Eva and Ennis Catalain had disappeared, leaving a hole that the town filled with the most convenient of stuffings—anger. The fact that Eva and Ennis' daughter Velda had grown up to be the loosest of women, and same with *her* daughters Ursula and Xenia, didn't help matters.

And it wasn't just the licentiousness of the Catalain women that spurred Meredith's distrust of them; it had been the life mission of Meredith's mother Midge to bring down the family. Midge believed with her very soul that the Catalains had gotten away with murder—the murder of Velda Catalain's husband, specifically. Allowing an act like that to go unpunished was akin to taking part in it.

Meredith had been weaned on these truths. Even so, she may have been content to nurture a low-burning resentment toward the Catalains, never taking up her mother's task to destroy them, if not for one thing: her husband Michael's "visit" to Ursula Catalain the year before Heather was born.

Meredith's desperation to get pregnant combined with the test results showing Michael had lazy sperm had goaded her into thrusting her husband into the arms of that Medusa. She assumed Michael and Ursula's affair began the night he bought the potion. Mixing business and pleasure would have been bad enough, except that over the course of their two-week affair, they'd had the poor taste to fornicate in public. Specifically, in Ursula's car in the ValuCo parking lot, Ursula's head popping up and down like a rocking horse. Meredith knew this because her best friend Caramine had witnessed it, and related the story to Meredith in great detail before sharing it with the entire town.

Meredith could never forgive the fact that she had planted the seeds of that affair, and worse, that she was beholden to Ursula for the birth of her daughter. (In the rare moment when she was completely honest with herself, she had to admit that it might be the fact that Ursula was *on top*—a position that Meredith herself had always been unwilling to take—that pricked the hardest.)

Meredith and Michael had never talked about the shameful tryst, and whenever she broached the idea of owing their only child to Ursula, he always laughed at her until, after two decades, she gave up mentioning it and replaced her resentment with religious zeal and an ongoing plan to destroy the Catalains where her mother had failed.

These life goals fit like gloves.

Except she'd discovered that Ursula was hard to get at. The woman stayed mostly in her cottage at the rear of her house, concocting her potions and sleeping with other women's husbands. Helena and Xenia, with their storefront, were easier, and so it was with a combination of boycotts, smear campaigns, and light vandalism that Meredith had been attacking the Seven Daughters almost since it had opened fourteen years ago, trying to destroy the Catalains the same way they'd upended her own life.

Unfortunately for Meredith, Helena and Xenia's reputation as honest businesspeople and the unique quality of their wares always won out. Helena knew this, just like she knew that Midge, Meredith's mother, had been right. Velda *had* murdered her own husband and gotten away with it. In addition, Helena knew that Ursula had slept with Meredith's spouse. So, she didn't take Meredith's vendetta personally, and in fact pitied her, always offering her and her lady friends candy and lemonade when they were picketing the store, hot chocolate if it was winter.

This was the first time, however, that Meredith had stepped foot inside Seven Daughters.

Her mouth was set so tight a razor wouldn't have fit through her lips.

Helena stopped in mid-inhale, frozen like a rabbit. The interior glass of her candy case fogged over, as if breathing for her. This wasn't good.

The fact that Meredith had entered the store meant her need for vengeance had ramped up. What could have set her off, especially considering Ursula was out of town? More importantly, how could Helena get rid of Meredith without angering her further? Xenia was still in the back room. Leo was boxing candy. The only other people in the store—two women, presumably from the tourist bus—were chatting obliviously over a rack of dresses.

Helena wasn't sure what to do, so she fell back on her standby: kindness.

"Welcome, Meredith!" After all the hours Meredith had devoted to her, Helena felt the least she could do was address her by her first name. "I'm so glad you finally came inside. Can I offer you some candy? Help you shop for a dress, perhaps? Or maybe you just wanted to say a quick 'hi?'"

Meredith scowled so deeply that she emitted the smell of sulfur. She prowled toward the candy counter. "I'm not here to buy anything."

"Oh?" The fog in the candy case cleared, revealing melted puddles of chocolate. Leo had turned from his work and was staring keenly at Meredith. Even the two women in the racks had stopped to pay attention.

"Don't play coy with me, Helena Catalain." Meredith's voice was low, ominous. The overhead lights flickered. Helena believed she caught the faint scent of vinegar coming from the corner where she had displayed the grape globe candy, matchhead-sized orbs of spun sugar clustered around an edible green vine. "I know what sort of magic you're up to in here, and I can *finally* do something about it."

Helena's world went black. She blinked rapidly until light returned and glanced at the two customers. They were watching the exchange uneasily. "Now Meredith," Helena said, her voice even but her knees shaking. "You're too kind. It's not magic that makes our candy and dresses so popular, but I appreciate your endorsement."

Xenia walked out of the back room, a yellow measuring tape in hand, two criss-crossed pencils holding up her salt-and-pepper bun.

"Sister, Meredith Baum has kindly paid us a visit!" Helena's voice was pitched too high.

Xenia cocked her head, a slow smile spreading across her angular face. Someone unfamiliar with her would have thought she was welcoming Meredith. Helena recognized the expression for what it was: a cat spotting a mouse.

"Meredith!" Xenia tossed the tape over her shoulder. "You've finally entered the witch's lair!"

Meredith turned as white as lefse. "I knew it," she hissed.

It took her a full thirty seconds to realize she was being made fun of. Xenia's laughter turned Meredith's shade to pink.

Helena felt terrible. Them being witches was another thing Meredith was right about, and no one would believe her. Helena was stepping around the case to console Meredith—she thought it cruel to laugh at others, no matter who they were—when the front door swung open, admitting a woman so wide she had to angle her shoulders to fit through. She lurched all the way to the candy counter, grabbing Meredith's arm as if for support. She was in her early 20s and out of breath.

"I'm tired of hiding!" Her hair was disheveled, sweaty blond curls plastered to her enormous face. Her hands were so plump that they looked like blown-up surgeon's gloves, and her shapeless sundress was straining to hold all her flesh.

But that's not what everyone was staring at.

A tattoo was etching itself into the top half of the arm that was holding Meredith, the woman's skin swelling with color and shape as sure as if a needle was puncturing her flesh.

The woman cried out in pain.

Meredith gasped.

Helena wondered how much worse this day could get.

Chapter 3

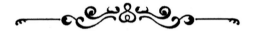

The enormous woman slapped her hand over her arm to cover the emerging tattoo.

Meredith shrunk back, wresting her arm away. "What *are* you?"

The woman blinked, crystal-ball tears sliding down her cheeks. "I'm Claudette."

The simple, heartbreaking beauty of the words crushed Helena. She rushed forward to hold Claudette, though her arms were barely long enough to reach the backs of her shoulders. "Welcome to the store, Claudette."

Claudette sniffled. "I didn't mean to come here. I went to the little shop in back of the Queen Anne? To get help from the...other one? But she wasn't there. I don't know how I ended up here."

Helena patted Claudette's shoulders. Taking the touch as encouragement, Claudette's story rolled out like marbles as the tattoo continued to stipple her skin, its shape emerging in waves:

She'd gone in search of Ursula this morning. Visiting the cottage behind the Queen Anne had been her piss-aller, something she never would have done if she hadn't been denied access to the plane last week. It was supposed to be a weekend getaway with her girlfriends, a spontaneous trip to Las Vegas. She'd never flown before. She'd been excited. Then she'd spotted her seat, about the size of a dinner plate. She tried squeezing in, and with a little prodding, she was successful. If that damn stewardess, herself so skinny she looked like two sticks rolled in hair, hadn't come by and insisted Claudette wear a seat belt, it would have worked fine.

As it was, they made her deplane and wait for a larger one to come along. She swore to her friends that she'd board it, but as soon as they took off, she drove home to Faith Falls. "A woman can only take so much shame, you know?"

Leo passed a tissue over the counter, and Helena handed it to Claudette. Her tears were pouring freely now, tender glass globes rolling down her cheeks and shattering against the wood floor. Xenia and the other two customers had gathered close, everyone in the store hypnotized by Claudette's story and the mysterious image emerging on her arm.

"It's not that I want to be thin," Claudette continued. "I just want to feel *safe*. Growing up with an alcoholic, handsy father took care of that, you know? Food became my out." Her voice grew faraway. "A juicy steak steeped in cream of mushroom soup sprinkled with French-fried onions makes me feel secure, at least while I eat it. Then I want bread with butter, and ice cream laced with toffee crumbles, and then sugar-sweet coffee, and then more, but it's never enough because eventually I have to stop eating and there's just me, and the judging world." Claudette inhaled a shaky breath.

The tattoo finished itself on her forearm at that moment. It was a vivid green snake wrapped three times around her arm, a salacious pink tongue licking out of its fanged mouth. Meredith spotted it, and the blood drained out of her face.

Another tattoo began carving itself on Claudette's exposed shoulder immediately after the first ended. She seemed oblivious to the pain of the second one, so caught up was she in her story.

"I'd heard of the witch on Hazel Street." Claudette glanced guiltily at Helena, and over at Xenia. "Everyone has. My mom even went to school with her, though she said she was normal back then. None of my friends have visited the Queen Anne cottage, but I knew a friend of a friend who'd gone because she had cold sores and wanted to be rid of them once and for all. The rumor had it that her cold sores disappeared but that her cat was run over the same month."

Claudette blew her nose with the tissue she'd been handed. "I don't own a cat, but I am prepared to pay a steep price to feel like the world has room for me." She stared at Meredith, who was listening to the whole story in horror. "I'm tired of people telling me I smell good or have pretty eyes or I'm funny, and I don't care if that makes me sound shallow."

She went quiet.

Xenia broke the silence. "You're missing something."

Claudette's eyebrows shot up.

"Those tattoos that are working their way out of your skin." Xenia pointed at Claudette's exposed upper arm. The second tattoo was nearly complete It was horrific, a lump of grey-green flesh with teeth and hair.

"No!" Helena yelled before she could stop herself. She threw an arm out to steady herself. "I mean, yes to Xenia's question. What about the tattoos?"

Claudette shrugged. "They started appearing after I left the Queen Anne. And then I found myself here."

"Do they hurt?" Leo asked.

Claudette nodded. "Terribly." She pointed at the now-complete tumor tattoo on her shoulder. "This is the third. I have another one on the front of my thigh. A jail cell with a skeleton in it. I thought a hive of bees was stinging me. What do you think they mean?"

Helena glanced around the circle. Shock was written on everyone's face but Xenia's, who looked more curious than anything. "I don't know," Helena said. "Ursula might know, but she won't be back until the end of the week." She didn't know what else to say, so she offered Claudette a wafer of a Money Luck bar from the sample plate on the counter. They were the only candy that hadn't been harmed by Meredith's vitriol. Claudette snatched the morsel like an antidote, popping it in her mouth and swallowing it whole.

"Do you like it?" Helena asked, smiling.

Claudette nodded. "It's delicious. But I think it's missing something."

Helena's hand flew to her heart. It wasn't that she minded healthy criticism. It was just that her candies had never before been less than perfect. She snatched the last emerald-dusted square from the sample plate and popped it in her mouth, rolling it around. She tasted the bittersweet chocolate, and the organic honey, and the almonds she'd ground almost to powder to add a nutty crunch. It was delicious and reminded her that she needed to put more of her money into savings. She opened her eyes, pleasure written across her face. "What could it possibly be missing?"

"Mint." There was certainty in Claudette's voice, but that's not what convinced Helena to hire her on the spot as her assistant. It was the *truth* of it. This candy needed a hint of mint, absolutely demanded it. Helena laughed a deep, throaty chuckle, wrapped her arm around Claudette, and walked her back to the kitchen, Meredith forgotten.

Meredith backed out of the store. If Helena had still been there to see it, she would have witnessed the transcendent glow of victory on Meredith's face, and it would have scared her to her bones. Whatever Meredith had come for, she had gotten it, and then some.

The ground under Faith Falls rumbled, but with a new tenor.

The snakes were talking. Soon, it would be time to rise.

The Catalain Book of Secrets: Embracing Uncertainty

Embracing uncertainty, also known as entertaining negative capability, is a useful skill. If you don't come by it naturally, here's a spell to help:

First, gather three votive candles and a match. Also, collect a pinch of dried chamomile, mugwort bud, and pansy petals. If you have tarot cards, remove The Star. If you do not have cards, simply draw a five-pointed star on a piece of paper.

1. Set the star in front of you.

2. Set the candles around you, within reach.

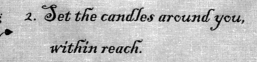

3.

4. Light the candles. Dust the first candle with the chamomile and say, "patience." Dust the second candle with the dried mugwort bud and say, "resilience." Finally, dust the third candle with the dried pansy petals and say, "knowledge."

5. Study the star. Inhale calm, exhale worry. Inhale calm, exhale worry. Inhale calm, exhale worry.

6. Close your eyes once you feel centered. Picture the uncertainty in your life. Hold it in your mind and heart as close as you would a lover. Feel the white light of gratitude surround you. Embrace it until the candles have burnt down. When you lose sight of your passion for the uncertainty, vision the candle and hear these words in your head "patience,

resilience, knowledge." Regather the uncertainty when you're able.

7. Once the candles are no longer burning, you will be full of peace and assured the best possible outcome.

*If you like, keep the star out where you can see it to remind yourself that you're in good hands.

CHAPTER 4

A light giddiness washed over Helena when she spotted Meredith outside Seven Daughters the next morning, picket sign in hand. Three other women were at her side, their signs exhorting people to "Shop with Your Conscience!" and "Support Families." The last one was vague, certainly, but familiar. And how serious could Meredith's visit yesterday have been if she was still following her same routine? Her entering the store and making vague threats must have been a fluke.

Hence the relief Helena felt, which was perfectly in line with the sweet hope of this spring morning. The sun was a trembling lemon, fighting to ship its heat to the town below. By noon, it would be at least 60 degrees, and the bright buds on the oaks and maples lining Main Street were paying attention. They shivered and stretched, waiting for the perfect moment to unfurl in a symphony of green. The only businesses open this early were the Homerun Café and Willmar's Drugstore, but at least a dozen people besides those outside of Seven Daughters were out and about, enjoying the lovely fresh air.

Helena hadn't been spotted by the picketers. She ducked into the entrance of Ren's Watches, Unique Timepieces Sold and Repaired, which wouldn't open until nine, to collect herself. She'd been in Seven Daughters until the wee hours, training a gifted Claudette in the art of candy-making. The woman was such a natural that Helena would have been jealous if she'd been anyone else. She was looking forward to working with Claudette again today, though Claudette refused to say whether or not she would come back. At least no more tattoos had appeared on her since the tumor.

A familiar word danced down the street and caught her ear—*Helena*. Meredith and friends were talking about her, and the clear morning breeze was carrying the words. She was trapped. It was bad to eavesdrop, but it was even worse for people to think you were eavesdropping, which Meredith would surely do if she caught Helena coming out from the entrance where she was hiding. She considered covering her ears, but she heard her own name again.

She leaned forward. She was only human, after all.

"…is so nice. Are you sure?"

"Sure she's a witch, if that's what you mean!" Helena recognized Meredith's voice. It was a gust blazing the brushfire, the latter fueled by the betrayal present since the moment Eva and Ennis had deserted Faith Falls, and coaxed even hotter by the open sexuality of the remaining Catalain women.

Helena recognized the next voice as belonging to Gladys Chanter, an accountant who used to take care of Seven Daughter's books until Ursula had screwed her husband. "Ursula is supposed to be out of town for a week. Did you all hear? Xenia and Helena can't possibly dodge this one without her."

An unfamiliar voice picked up the outrage. "I heard that Ursula is on a recruiting mission across Minnesota, searching for young women to teach the dark arts to."

"I believe it," Gladys said. "And Xenia? She was holding hands in public with another woman. She'll be the death of decency if she isn't already."

That was exactly enough. Helena marched out, fully intending to give the four women a piece of her mind. They didn't spot her until she was almost on top of them. She was going to do it. She was finally going to give someone a piece of her mind, and it was about time.

"Helena," Meredith said, a superior smile creeping across her face. Her copper hair was yanked back into a severe bun. "I was telling the ladies about the interesting day at your store yesterday."

Helena opened her mouth. She wanted to tell them that her sister was the kindest heart she'd ever met and above reproach, despite her sometimes prickly exterior, that all that had happened at the store yesterday was a poor woman who'd received more than her share of curses, and anyway, whose business was it if she and her family were witches, and in fact, why didn't more women try a little witchcraft? But her lips wouldn't form those words, as much as they wanted to. Instead, she said, "I'm sorry."

Meredith's eyebrows shot up. "For what?"

"For how unhappy you are, and for any harm my family has ever done to yours." Helena felt the tears push up, angry tears at words unspoken, but she couldn't bring herself to say the rest. *But that gives you no right to hurt us.*

Helena stumbled toward the front door of Seven Daughters, unlocked it, and stepped inside the cool room. On the other side of the door, she inhaled deeply. She welcomed the sweet dust her chocolates left in the air, the crisp smell of cottons and silks, the bitter undertones of burnt sugar. Nerves settled, she set about getting the store ready for opening in an hour, trying as hard as she could not to think about Gladys Chanter's words:

Xenia and Helena can't possibly dodge this one without her.

Which one? What was there to dodge?

When Xenia arrived a half an hour later, Helena accepted the peck on her cheek without her usual smile, but she didn't tell Xenia about the encounter, or her growing fear that Meredith finally had something on them.

"What is it?"

A smile peeped at the corners of Helena's mouth. Who had she been kidding? She'd never been particularly good at hiding things from her sister. That didn't mean she would tell her the worries she had about Meredith, however. No need to borrow trouble. But she could talk to Xenia about something else that had been bothering her.

"Do you ever wish our life had been different?"

The laugh startled out of Xenia's mouth. "How so?"

Helena set down the spatula she'd been stirring the gelée with. She'd peeled, pitted, sliced, and boiled 3 pounds of fresh peaches to create the base. "That we hadn't come back to Faith Falls, for starters."

Xenia dipped her finger in the mix and shrugged. "No changing that." She studied the stickiness on the tip of her finger—it was as orange as the sun—before tucking it in her mouth. "Delicious! Did you add lime juice?"

Helena nodded. Xenia wasn't in the mood to talk, which was fine. She at least was no longer worrying about what was bothering Helena. Helena gave her a spontaneous hug and then returned to her confections.

So immersed in candy-making was she that she would have missed witnessing Xenia fall in love for the first time in her life if her timer hadn't gone off at just the right moment. She'd turned the oven off and cracked the door, marveling at the gorgeous cumulous cloud meringue puffs she'd been baking. They were Xenia's favorite dessert, so she went to retrieve her sister before the meringues moved past the chewy phase. It was a small window, maybe two minutes.

She was stepping through the kitchen door, her sister's name on her lips, when the sight of the gorgeous woman just inside the door stopped her in her tracks. She was an exotic creature, her head heavy with black, gold, and copper dreadlocks laced with jewels and metal rings. Her eyes were amber-green tiger eyes, but one stared off another direction than the other.

Her body curved like a cello, and she moved with a dancer's grace. If her eyes had treated each other like sisters, she would be so stunning that she'd be difficult to look at. As it was, the visual defect was too pronounced, and such a contrast to her beauty, that an average person would be inclined to feel immediately superior when looking at her, as if it was preferable to be unexceptional than to fly so close to the sun and fail.

Her face wore a lost expression.

"Can I help you?" Xenia's voice was husky.

Neither woman noticed Helena, who smelled something spicy and secret with a hint of primrose. Xenia, who had stood up from her sewing machine, must have smelled it, too. Helena swallowed the gasp when the amber-colored perfume visibly worked itself like a kiss up Xenia's spine, to the small of her neck, under her earlobes, caressing her nose and lips.

"I was supposed to meet a friend here," the woman said. A line developed between her gorgeous tiger eyes, one staring around the store in concern, the other aimed at Xenia. "I've been waiting outside for fifteen minutes, and she still hasn't shown. Those picketers are making me uncomfortable. Could I use your phone?"

"Of course." Xenia indicated the front counter where the old-fashioned black dial phone rested. Helena worried they would see her standing feet from the phone, but both were oblivious to anything but one another. A heat built in Helena's heart and pushed out through her mouth as a smile. Here was true love, happening right in front of her.

How lucky am I!

The woman dialed, her eyes peeking into every corner of the store at once, skittering over Helena but not stopping anywhere save on Xenia. The whirr click of the dial returning to rest after each number sounded to Helena like a timer counting down to the beginning of something. The woman held the phone to her ear for two minutes before hanging up.

"I'm sorry," she said, to no one in particular.

Xenia set down the empire-waisted, knee-high dress exactly the shade of tawny green as the woman's eyes. "No answer?"

The woman shook her head and continued to gape around the store as if awaking from a dream. "Can you believe I've never been inside here before? I've walked by a hundred times, and I never even entered."

Xenia walked forward and held out her hand. "I'm Xenia."

The woman held out hers. "Cleo."

When their skin touched, a snap of electricity jumped between them, raising Xenia's short hairs and making the brass clasps in Cleo's hair hum.

"You sell dresses and candy?" Cleo hadn't let go of Xenia's hand.

"That's it."

The woman kept one eye steady on Xenia, and the other kept spinning. "Did you design your own dress?"

"I did," Xenia said, glancing down at the simple batik shift she wore over leggings and a pair of leather ballet flats. She preferred her clothing comfortable, and in jewel tones. "I could sew you one. If you'd like."

Cleo pulled her hand from Xenia's and put it to her throat. She seemed sad. "I don't think I was supposed to come inside."

"You don't have to stay. I have something I'd like to show you, though." Xenia held up a green-gold dress. She had been working on it for over a week, longer than she spent on most. She'd confessed to dreams about it, lucid memories of a woman wearing the dress like a mermaid, shimmering and swimming, shades of deepest green and sea blue mixing with the fine flow of sunlight.

Cleo grabbed the rack of dresses nearest her for support. "It's lovely."

Helena felt a little faint herself. She was used to the brilliance of her sister's work, but this dress was something else, something so alive it felt like a proposal. She wasn't surprised when Cleo walked backward toward the door, hands feeling behind her. She could neither take her eyes off the dress nor stay this close to the glory of it. She stumbled outside without another word.

Xenia watched her go, unmoving.

"The dress is stunning," Helena said. "So beautiful it blinded her."

"*She* was beautiful," Xenia whispered, almost as if she was talking to herself. "This dress is meant for her."

Helena nodded. That much was obvious. "Are you going to ask her out?"

Xenia set the dress down as if waking from a dream, but when she turned to Helena, her green Catalain eyes were laser-focused. "Certainly. If you agree to go out with Artemis."

Underground, the snakes stopped rumbling for a nanosecond, shivering with something akin to laughter.

The Catalain Book of Secrets:
Accepting Good Love

Most Catalain women are born with
skew-whiff pickers. Specifically,
when it comes to choosing lovers, they are
attracted to the unhealthy and put off by
the open-hearted. If you find your picker is
off, follow these steps to reset it:

1. Purchase two rose quartz hearts and two
   pink candles, votives preferred. Also, place
   a white pillowcase on your favorite pillow
   and obtain a single red rose, removing the
   petals. Discard the stem.

2. On the night of the next full moon, slide
   the rose quartz hearts under your pillow
   and sprinkle the rose petals on top of it.
   Light the pink candles at the foot of
   your bed, making sure they cannot
   tip or burn anything around them.

3. Lay on the rose petals. Watch the candles flicker. As they burn down, feel the warmth of true love in your heart. See yourself in the flames, with an anonymous lover, feeling valued and cherished. (*Caution: do not envision a specific person. This is dangerous if you possess a cockeyed picker because you risk binding the bad seed to yourself. If s/he enters your mind, push them out, using two fingers to make a snipping motion over your heart as if a scissors is cutting a rotten bind. Repeat as often as necessary.)

4. Fall asleep naturally, either before or after the candles burn out.

5. When next you wake, your picker will no longer be cockeyed. Unfortunately, your brain will test this like your tongue worries a sore tooth, so be on your guard for a bad seed to make one last attempt to burn your heart.

CHAPTER 5

"Shall I?"

Artemis X. Buckley stood on the front porch of the Queen Anne. His hair was slicked back and his moustache and beard were trimmed. He wore a pressed white cotton shirt, dark green slacks, and polished shoes. He clutched his fedora in his right hand. A tourmaline breeze rolled over his shoulders and kissed Helena on the earlobes. It smelled of thawing earth and cherry SweeTarts. The caress made her smile, as did the wrist corsage he held out to her. The centerpiece was a hothouse lily, white and honeyed, surrounded by daffodils the color of lemon pie and tiny blue hyacinth buds.

"It's beautiful." Helena held her hand out. Artemis slipped the band around her wrist. When his warm hands brushed hers, she yelped.

"Did I give you a shock?"

"Something like that." She hurried ahead of him so he wouldn't see her blush. So what if his touch had shot electricity to every tip of her? That was no reason to act like a schoolgirl. In fact, it was crucial that she keep her head and heart on straight. She wasn't going to fall for Artemis, certainly not. He was dating her mother. She was simply eating a meal with him as it was the only way Xenia would agree to ask Cleo out.

"I mentioned I am only interested in a friendship?" Helena asked. She could be forthright when it involved respecting someone else's feelings.

"Three times," Artemis said agreeably, "and that's only since I showed up on your porch."

Helena searched for sarcasm in his words and found none. In fact, if she was pressed, she would say the only discernible emotion had been humor. *He's welcome to think it's funny. I don't believe people's feelings are a laughing matter.*

Still, the smell of the lily on her wrist was intoxicating, and when Artemis placed his hand in the small of her back to guide her into his vehicle, she just barely bit back a second happy squeal. His car, a perfectly-preserved 1954 green Cadillac Eldorado, was as clean inside as out, the leather seats a pale cream color that hugged Helena and made her feel even prettier in her pale blue Angora sweater and loose white slacks.

As if reading her mind, Artemis complimented her as he slid behind the wheel. "I've never seen you look better." He paused, and Helena swore she detected a chuckle in his next words. "For a friend, that is."

"Thank you." She rested her purse on her lap. The night was glorious, with a full moon glowing the crisp-cool edges of the evening. This warm and early spring had the plants and the bees thrumming with excitement, and it was contagious. Helena felt a thread of warning running through the hope, a distant memory of something dark that came hand-in-hand with this unusual weather, but she pushed the sensation toward the back. Why worry about something that wasn't here? How could such a thing even be possible with the people of Faith Falls lining the streets of downtown, laughing, holding hands, and smiling at anything that moved?

Artemis drove toward downtown Faith Falls, steering the Eldorado into two parking spaces in front of Amore Buono, the Italian restaurant that had opened on the corner behind Hobbes Theater three months earlier. Helena's eyes widened. She'd heard the food was wonderful, but that it was impossible to secure a reservation. She'd also heard it was expensive.

"I don't mind burgers," she blurted. She slapped her hand over her mouth. She suspected Artemis was not a rich man, and she didn't want him to put himself out. She hadn't intended to be so blunt about it.

He didn't hide his chuckle this time as he leaned into the steering wheel, his hands at ten o'clock and two o'clock. When he turned to Helena, she noticed that his eyes weren't just brown, they were the color of rich dark chocolate.

"I don't mind burgers, either," he said, "but tonight I'm craving Italian. I could see if they have burgers on the menu?"

She shook her head, her gray-blonde curls falling into her face. She didn't even know why she'd bothered doing her hair tonight. "I'm being silly. Pasta would be wonderful."

And it was. As were the Chianti, and the tiramisu, and the cannoli, and the violin player Artemis called over to their table, and even worse, so was the conversation. Artemis was a simple man, born in the cabin on Rum River that he had remodeled to become his current home. He'd never been married, had no children. He liked to work with wood, said it "talked" to him, told him what it wanted to be, and that he was more of a facilitator than a carpenter. He liked to fish, took one trip a year to visit an aunt in Arizona, and he liked to read.

Best of all, he listened more than he talked, and Helena found herself revealing secrets she'd never told anyone but her sister: how she'd stolen a pair of earrings from Velda when she was seven but felt so guilty she never left Velda's bedroom with them. Velda had found Helena giving herself a time out in the corner when she returned home. She shared that Xenia was on a date of her own, and so Leo was closing the store alone for the first time.

She confessed her fears that Xenia would die before her, that her sister would fall in love and that she wouldn't, that someday her magic would be gone and her candy would taste like nothing more than its ingredients.

Artemis nodded through all of it, asked questions when she paused, and laughed at the funny parts. Helena grew warmer, and it wasn't just the wine.

"You're an interesting man, Artemis X. Buckley," she finally said, when she felt empty of stories. It was a good feeling, like opening a savings account with money you didn't even know you had.

"And you're a magical woman, Helena."

Helena glanced around. To her surprise, the restaurant was nearly empty. They'd closed the place. "Look at this! I can't believe we've stayed out this late."

Artemis reached across the table. Helena saw his hand coming toward her and wanted so badly to take it. But she couldn't. She shouldn't even be on a date with this man who was courting her mother. She knew the rest of the Catalain women wouldn't mind, were surprised she hadn't already crossed that line, in fact. She also suspected that Artemis knew the Catalain reputation, which is why he was here. She suddenly wanted to leave, very badly.

She stood abruptly. She hadn't intended for her chair to fall over, but it did. She reached for it but was overcome by an excruciating pain in her left chest and arm, a hundred burning needles boring into her flesh. "No!"

Artemis was at her side in an instant. He righted the chair and eased her into it. "What is it? Is it your heart?"

Beads of perspiration broke along her hairline. A worried waiter hovered in the periphery. She hated to worry people like this. She inhaled deeply. The pain would pass. It always did.

"Pulled muscle," she said through gritted teeth. "Sorry to make such a fuss."

Artemis' eyes narrowed. "Pulled muscle?"

She heard it in his voice. He knew she was lying. She couldn't bear to look him in the eye, and so she reached for her purse with her right hand and forced herself to stand. Planting her best impression of a smile on her face, she walked toward the door. She wanted to pay her share, but she needed fresh air.

By the time Artemis joined her on the sidewalk outside the restaurant, she was herself again. The pain had left a gray shadow that made it difficult to move her left arm, but she knew from experience that that, too, would recede soon. At least she hoped. The pain had never been this bad.

"Thank you for dinner!" she said brightly.

Artemis stood in front of her. She was not a tall woman, but his eyes barely met hers, and they were unflinching. "That was no pulled muscle. You don't have to tell me what it was, but I ask you to tell someone."

She tried a laugh. It sounded genuine to her ears. "If it gets worse, I promise I will," she said. *Because I couldn't stand it if it got worse.*

He watched her for another heartbeat and then nodded before walking toward the car to open her door. Helena liked that he didn't treat her with kid gloves.

She tried to return the conversation to its previous depth, but the connection was lost. She'd lied to Artemis, and that was that. "Do you mind stopping by the store on the way home? I want to make sure Leo shut everything down okay."

It was her second lie of the night. She trusted Leo. She just didn't want Artemis to go quite yet.

"Of course."

Two blocks later, they were outside the store.

So was Leo.

"Oh no!" Helena pulled the door open. He should have gone home hours earlier. Her heart thudded in her ribcage. She raced toward him. "Is it Xenia?"

Leo shook his head. He was a thin boy, but he appeared particularly gaunt tonight, toplit by a streetlamp, his cheeks drawn and his eyes sunken. He held a packet of papers toward Helena.

"Meredith dropped these off. She said to give them to you or Xenia, whoever I saw first."

"And you've been standing here the whole time, hoping one of us would stop by? I'm sure it could have waited until tomorrow."

He shook his head by way of answer. His face dropped even further into his shoulders.

Helena's eyes shot to the papers. Her mouth went dry. They looked official. She rifled through them, not understanding what she was reading.

"They're eminent domain papers," Leo said, his voice a husk. "Meredith says the city is going to build a park where the Queen Anne is right now, that it's the only place that'll work. She also said the store is tied to the Queen Anne. If one goes, they both go."

The Catalains are going to lose everything.

Helena wasn't sure if Leo said the words or she just heard them in her head. She now knew what Meredith had been so smug about when she entered the store two days ago, and what she'd been talking about with the picketers just the other day. She finally, really did have something on them. "Don't tell Xenia."

Artemis coughed. "I've always believed that if you have a problem, you tell your family. Especially if it involves them."

Leo didn't answer. He didn't have to. His eyes were pleading with Helena to listen to Artemis.

"Of course I'll tell Xenia. I just want it to come from me, and not from anyone else. Understood?" Her voice was firm. She wished the same were true of her knees.

Artemis didn't respond but Leo seemed almost relieved. "You'll tell Xenia, then? And Ursula, when she gets back?"

"Of course." *Just as soon as I figure out how.*

The Catalain Book of Secrets:
Inertia Antidote

While it is commonly understood that an object in motion stays in motion, most folks are less comfortable acknowledging that a passive person stays inert unless a powerful enough force dictates otherwise. If you know it's time to act and would rather not wait for the 2 x 4 solution the Universe is sure to provide, follow this spell:

1. Buy or make smelling salts. To make them, combine ¼ cup Epsom salt, 1 tablespoon kosher salt, and two drops each of the following essential oils: eucalyptus, peppermint, and lemongrass. Stir the mixture with a disposable wooden stick, then seal in a glass pint jar.

2. Write down what it is you know you need to do.

3. Read it out loud three times.

4. Smell the salts.

5. Do what you need to do. You will not fail.

*If time is of the essence, skip steps 1-4. But, you already knew that.

CHAPTER 6

Black and red nightmares slashed Helena's sleep. She woke at 5:23 the next morning, overcome with guilt. She had to tell Xenia about the eminent domain papers. She jumped out of bed. She must act before her fear had a chance to catch her. Padding barefoot down the cool hall, she knew she wasn't moving fast enough. The cold oil of inertia whispered through her blood, promising her everything would be better if she simply pushed the negative from her mind. Thinking about bad things made them real, and final. Compartmentalizing the bad into a tiny closet in the corner of her heart, though, left all sorts of room for good things, bright things that made her laugh and hope.

Yet, she fought on. If she stopped to knock, she'd chicken out. She barged into Xenia's room, blinking until her eyes adjusted. Piles of fabric confused her. Were those lumps Xenia? There was no dawn yet, only a lessening of darkness. She stumbled toward the four-poster bed.

"Xenia?"

No answer. She poked the shape under the quilt. It gave. Pulling back the comforter, she saw only a mound of pillows. Xenia must not have returned from her date last night. Something like relief but closer to the comfort of a bad habit breathed over Helena. It wasn't time to tell Xenia yet. If it had been, she'd have been here. The same went for Ursula.

That was it! Why hadn't she thought of that before? When Ursula returned, which should be tomorrow, or the day after at the latest, she'd sit both her and Xenia down and show them the papers. No point in telling them separately.

Her shoulders relaxed. She made her way to the bathroom and showered, careful as always not to look down as she washed herself. Afterward, she dried herself off and slipped on a nutmeg-colored jersey dress that would allow her to move freely as she baked. She ate a breakfast of oatmeal, coffee, bacon, and grapes. She wore a smile as she drove into work.

The grin widened when she spotted Claudette outside the door. It was a school day, so Leo wouldn't be in until 3:30. No telling when Xenia would show up. Helena would need the help.

"Good morning!"

Claudette waved, keeping her hand close to her side. When Helena neared, she spotted a new tattoo, an ugly thing wrapped around Claudette's neck just about her t-shirt collar like a demon ferret. She tried to look away, to pretend to fumble for her keys, but it was too late.

"Horrible, isn't it?"

Helena stuck the key in the slot, still not looking at Claudette. "I'm not sure what you're talking about." She was a terrible liar, but at the rate she was going and if practice made perfect, she'd be a pro by the end of the week.

"It's okay," Claudette said. The effort to walk from the sidewalk to the door had her out of breath. "I'm getting used to them. This one came after a little boy brushed up against me at the supermarket. I had to leave my groceries in the cart and walk out because it hurt so bad. They say the neck is the worst, but it can't be as bad as the...never mind."

Helena held the door open for Claudette. She patted Claudette's back as the woman passed by, huffing sideways to get in. The tattoo began to appear just below the ferret almost instantly, just as Helena had suspected. This one wasn't her tumor, though. It was the saddest sketch of Xenia, that much was clear even from the beginning lines. Claudette swatted at it.

Helena cleared her throat. "It's the deepest fears of those who touch you, isn't it? Your tattoos, I mean."

Claudette turned, blinking as Helena flicked on the lights and washed the store in fluorescence. She nodded. "I had a guess when you got woozy at the gnarly tumor that inked me after you touched me, but I was sure yesterday when I bumped up against the cutest guy," she said. "You know what tattoo carved itself onto the top of my foot? An almost perfect picture of him and me, in bed together, with other people watching."

She spoke matter-of-factly, but the words punched Helena. She couldn't help herself. She stepped forward and squeezed Claudette as tightly as she could. She didn't care what fears showed themselves on the woman. "People can be cruel."

"It wasn't his fault." Claudette's voice was muffled, her face crushed in Helena's embrace. "He can't help what his worst fear is. It's not like he said it out loud."

Helena stepped back, but Claudette stopped her before she could speak. "Don't even tell me that I have a kind heart, or that I have a pretty face for a fat girl," Claudette said, "or that I'm not fat. I know I am. And I don't care. I like food, it likes me. I just want to be okay hanging out with myself, you know? I want to be safe and solid." She shook her head as if reminiscing. "I knew I was in trouble even before I got kicked off that plane. The salad dressing told me."

Helena's hand flew to her throat. "Salad dressing? It talks to you?"

"Yep. In a way, anyhow. Stress sneaks up on me, and when it gets too bad, I have panic attacks. I usually catch it before it gets to that level, but not always. My best 'impending stress overload' indicator is how much salad dressing I have in my pantry. A bottle or two, and I'm fine. This last time, I had *thirteen* in there before I noticed." Her eyes widened, amazed at her own confession.

Helena shook her head. "I still don't get it. What's wrong with salad dressing?"

Claudette began to rumble toward the kitchen. "It's not the dressing itself. The dressing is only the canary in the coal mine. I start to get really stressed, and I tell myself it's time to diet. My brain equates diet with salad, and so I start to pick up salad dressing when I'm out shopping, and I don't even notice. The more salad dressing, the more stressed I am. *Thirteen*."

A tiny grin played with the corners of Helena's mouth. Claudette fit in the Catalain world perfectly. Helena might even have to tell her about PINCing, short for "Pretend It's Not Crazy," something all the Catalain women had done for each other at least once. Her favorite PINCing was when her niece Jasmine, not more than six at the time, had decided the Queen Anne was haunted. She wasn't worried about herself, only her four-year-old sister, Katrine. She waited until Katrine was asleep before dusting her in baby powder every night for a month. When asked about it, she'd said, "the ghost won't take her if they think she's one of theirs."

Ursula had wanted to put an end to it, but Helena had convinced her to PINC Jasmine, even though the girl was young for it. She'd naturally outgrown the urge to powder her sister, though she'd earned more than her share of PINCs since then, Helena knew.

"Well, I'm glad you listened to the salad dressing," Helena said. "Otherwise, you wouldn't be here, and I need your help."

Claudette's eyes lit up. "Lemme know what I can do."

A shyness skirted Helena. She'd been experimenting with a new truffle recipe, something she was calling Pops. The ingredients were basic, so far consisting of a sassafras vanilla center dipped in milk chocolate. Yet, it was one of her most challenging candies to craft—a chameleon candy. She needed to mix it just right so it would taste like the favorite childhood soda pop of whoever ate it. The flavors must be perfectly balanced to coax out the explorer's joy everyone had been born with but most lost along the way.

"Would you…would you try a new candy of mine? I can't seem to get it just right."

Claudette's laugh rolled out. "Is the Pope Catholic?"

"Oh good." Helena led her to the rear of the kitchen, moderating her walk so Claudette didn't have to hurry. "It's in the fridge."

She pulled out the tray of truffles and offered it to Claudette. "They're still too runny. I can't get the center just right. That's why I have to keep them refrigerated."

Claudette plucked the largest and popped it in her mouth whole. Her eyes closed in ecstasy. She let it sit on her tongue for several moments before chewing. Her eyes shot open in surprise. "Dreamsicle! And rootbeer. And…grape soda?" She giggled, a child's innocent laugh, full of curiosity and skinned knees and secret handshakes. Then she coughed, and the laugh disappeared. "And burp. Why does it taste like burp?"

"I know." Helena slid the tray back into the fridge. "I don't know what to take away to get rid of that closing flavor. There's only three ingredients in the center as it is. Sassafras, vanilla, and sugar."

"Take away?" Claudette shook her head, her eyes vibrating as if skimming an interior mental list. "You need to add something. That burp tasted old. You need a brightener in there, something to youth that final note. It needs to be unexpected, like the candy equivalent of a joy buzzer or a whoopee cushion. Saffron, maybe? Cumin?" She hummed to herself as she searched the enormous spice rack, selecting and discarding several.

A warmth spread through Helena. Claudette was a genius. Pops would be the best candy yet. The ding of the front door pulled her out of her gratitude state. *Forgot to lock it after we came in. Who would be out this early?* Panic immediately replaced the warmth. Was it Meredith? Helena hadn't had time to read through all the papers yet, though they were stuffed in her purse so she could scour them over lunch. They couldn't take the store so quickly, could they?

Xenia's laughter filtered through the door, and Helena's shoulders relaxed out of her ears. Her sister must have entered through the front door. And it didn't sound like she was alone. Helena couldn't wait to hear how the date had gone.

"Good morning." The swinging kitchen door tapped Helena's bottom.

Xenia was glowing, hand in hand with Cleo. "Good morning! You remember Cleo?"

"Of course." Helena smiled. Cleo still appeared a little lost, and Helena wanted to put her at ease. "How are you?"

"Good. But I need to be going." She pecked Xenia on the cheek. The racks of dresses rustled happily. "I'll call." She walked out, glancing back at the inside of the store once, her gorgeous, mismatched tiger eyes rolling into every corner.

When she was out of sight, Xenia sighed. "I'm in love."

"I can tell. What about her?"

"What do you mean?"

"She looked unsure."

Xenia pushed her hair back. "I'm her first woman. We're going to take it slow. But I think she's the one." The dresses whispered again. It was a happy sound.

"Your art agrees," Helena said. "And so do I. You're going to invite her to the Equinox party?"

By way of answer, Xenia turned toward the street and her eyes narrowed. "She's out early. Again."

Helena followed her gaze. Meredith was out front, alone. Helena's heart iced over. Was Meredith coming in by herself, to make sure Leo had given them the paperwork? Xenia would be so angry to find out that Helena already knew. A cold sweat broke out along Helena's upper lip. She opened her mouth and tried to push the words out. They wouldn't come. She reached for Xenia, who was walking toward the door. She grabbed the cotton of her dress. Xenia turned, a question on her face.

"Meredith. She—"

Outside, another woman stepped next to Meredith, and a second, then a third. One of them held up a sign. It was just a regular picket. Meredith must be keeping it up out of habit, right until the bitter end. Helena breathed out a long breath.

"Yes?" Xenia asked. "Meredith what?"

"She is picketing the store."

Xenia pursed her lips. "I see that." She studied her sister for a long moment, but whatever question was in her head never made it to her mouth. "And I'm sick of it. It's time to act."

"No!"

"Don't worry," Xenia said. "It'll just be a little curse, something to make them uncomfortable while they're out there. Might as well. They've spent plenty hours making our customers itchy over the years. And I'm feeling full of piss and vinegar this morning."

Helena shook her head so hard that her reading glasses fell off their perch in her hair. "You know a curse always comes back to you."

Claudette joined them in the main room, a jar of coriander in her hand. "I say curse 'em."

Xenia nodded approvingly. "It's two against one, Helena. I'm tired of waiting for bad luck to come to us. I'm going to meet it head on." She stepped to the door and tugged it open, a curious Claudette on her heels. She spoke three short words and flung them at the picketers.

Meredith may or may not have heard the words. If she did, she most certainly didn't understand them. Yet, their power smacked her, and she hit back. Dropping her sign, she raced toward Xenia and shoved her backward. Meredith's fellow picketers were too shocked to move, but Claudette caught Xenia before she hit the floor. The tattoo began to ink Claudette's cheek before she had a chance to catch her breath. It was a quick and short piece, two intersecting lines.

A cross.

Xenia saw it and laughed.

The Catalain Book of Secrets: Casting a Curse

Justice is slow. Curses are not. To cast a curse, choose the single word that best describes the discomfort you want your target to feel. Choose that word carefully—inconvenience, frustration, pain, the like—as every spell you cast will come back to you threefold. Once you have the curse word, aim your eyes, mouth, and heart at the one you mean to curse, and whisper "vomica pestis pestis." Follow that with the single word you have chosen.

It is done.

Settle in for the backlash.

CHAPTER 7

The curse wasn't instantly visible, but the next morning as Helena walked past Meredith outside Seven Daughters, she couldn't ignore the cloudiness in Meredith's right eye. It was milky, a skin of cotton over moist flesh. Seeing it made Helena's stomach hurt, and she couldn't stop glancing through the window throughout the day. Meredith kept blinking as she prowled the front sidewalk of the store, picket sign in hand. Helena didn't know if the cloud was painful or just made it difficult for Meredith to see.

She recognized it as Xenia's curse.

She turned away from the front of the store and spotted Claudette watching her. Helena stopped herself from startling, just.

"It's freeing, you know?"

Helena's cheeks warmed with embarrassment. When Claudette had arrived at work today, her entire face was covered in tattoos. Xenia's cross over her cheek, a clever shading around her eyes that looked as if a mask was being pulled off, an outline of a bullet hole in her temple, the silhouette of a naked woman on stage on her opposite cheek. Helena had not been able to hide the gasp when she'd first spotted the new tattoos, but she thought she'd gotten better at hiding her recurring shock since then.

"I've always been worried about what people think about me," Claudette continued. "Not anymore. It's all out there."

Helena nodded. She saw where Claudette's affliction was easier on her in some ways than it was on those who accidentally touched her. Leo had stopped by the store last night during close and brushed against Claudette on his way to the kitchen. To his naked-faced horror, a perfect 50s pin-up etched itself onto Claudette's bicep, black and white except for the red rosebud lips. He'd grown so pale that Helena had been worried he'd fall over. Xenia had laughed. Claudette seemed almost proud.

Helena wondered if Claudette had simply found a new layer to hide behind.

"I'm happy you're here," Helena told Claudette. She didn't know what else to say. Returning to the kitchen, she cooked throughout the day, letting Claudette work the counter. Xenia hummed as she sewed, likely thinking of Cleo. When the day ended, and Xenia drove her back to the Queen Anne, Helena realized she had never done less work and been more tired in her life.

She was washing the supper dishes when she cried out.

Xenia was leaning into the fridge, putting away the leftover hotdish. She dropped it in alarm, and the glass container fell to the floor, shattering. "What is it?"

Helena slumped over the sink, her left arm clutched to her chest.

"What's wrong?" When Helena didn't answer, couldn't, Xenia called for an ambulance. They let her ride alongside Helena, caressing her hair as they stabbed a needle in the back of her hand and checked her blood pressure and temperature.

Helena's pain ebbed before they arrived at the hospital. Xenia didn't stop stroking her sister's hair, but her face relaxed. Her relief turned itself inside out when Helena removed her shirt in the curtained treatment room and revealed the puckered black-and-yellow bruising that circled her left breast like a storm cloud before disappearing into her armpit. Helena yanked the hospital gown over the injury, but it was too late.

Xenia's voice was dry and tight. "What happened?"

Helena wouldn't meet her eyes. There was no more hiding, not here in the antiseptic lights, but she still tried. "It's been there a while. I must have fallen out of bed one night."

"On your tit?" Xenia asked.

Helena shrugged. Xenia rushed in and gathered her into a hug. She had to be coaxed into releasing her sister when the doctor arrived.

He was young, too young to be dissecting grown women for a living. "I'm Dr. Carter."

Helena recited her symptoms—six months' worth of pain and bruising extending from her left breast to her armpit, culminating in the excruciating attack of agony when she'd been washing dishes—and removed her gown for him. His face revealed nothing.

"Does this hurt?" Dr. Carter pressed at the edges of the bruises, so softly that the skin barely ruckled. Helena winced. Tears leaked out her eyes.

He nodded. "I'm sorry. I'll be as gentle as possible. Normally with these symptoms I'd order a mammogram, but given the level of pain, I'm going to send you for an MRI."

"Mammogram?" Xenia asked, her voice high.

"It's cancer," Helena said with quiet certainty. She kept her eyes on the floor, but humiliation was written across her face. It was out, no longer her secret to protect. She felt like she'd failed somehow.

Xenia put her arm on her sister's right shoulder. "You don't know that."

Helena didn't argue.

"That's what we'd like to rule out." Dr. Carter wrote as he spoke. He left the room, and a nurse returned to begin the gamut of tests.

Helena's breast cancer was diagnosed in less than three hours.

Because of the aggressiveness of the cancer, a double mastectomy was recommended. Helena agreed, numb to her very core. Her surgery was scheduled within the week. The prognosis was mixed. Ursula hurried home. Velda rushed to the hospital, as did Leo and Artemis, and Helena's nieces, Jasmine and Katrine, and Jasmine's daughter Tara.

With her family and friends gathered around, Helena conceded that she'd known about the cancer for a while. It had felt like heartache. She was ashamed that she'd allowed it into her body and so had lived with it like a stranger.

She chose to introduce herself to her cancer right before her oncologist removed it. She'd come to understand that it was a stumbling child grown too fast, unaware how much damage it was doing. She met it, apologized to it, loved and cradled it, and released it.

It had been a part of her for so long that she wondered if she could survive without it.

Then, she was wheeled into surgery.

The Catalain Book of Secrets:
Overcoming Shame

Once upon a time, there was a woman so ashamed that she hadn't chewed her food well enough that she allowed herself to quietly choke to death rather than interrupt dinner. The moral? Shame is deadly. It's a slow-acting poison. We can administer it to others but it's most dangerous when we swallow it ourselves. If you have accidentally ingested shame, you need to act quickly before it seeps into your bones. Do the following:

1. Write your shame down on a heart-shaped piece of paper.

2. Show the shame to one other person. Choose carefully. If you have friend or family that you trust, choose one of them.

If you do not have someone close whom you can trust with this, choose an acquaintance or a stranger with a good heart. They are everywhere.

3. Accept whatever gift they give you in return for your secret. It may not look like a gift at first, but it will be. Thank them.

4. Smile, no matter how you feel. If you can force yourself to laugh, do so.

The bubble of shame is pierced. You will see immediate, positive change, but be gentle with yourself. You've peeled off rotten armor, and the world will feel raw for a bit.

Chapter 8

When Helena regained consciousness, she felt like she'd survived a shark attack. Barely. First one eye opened, then the other. She was afraid to move anything else. It took her vision a moment to unblur. The honey-colored spring sunlight trickled through the hospital curtains, the air smelling like orange juice and rubbing alcohol. Outside in the hall, the murmur of nurses and clatter of attendants provided a steady hum.

There was no avoiding it any longer, so she took inventory of her body. Her toes wiggled, and she could move her legs side to side. She had a catheter inserted and so had no sensation of a full bladder. Her stomach was queasy.

Her breasts were gone.

Her glorious, powerful, feminine breasts.

"Good afternoon."

She whipped her head to the right. The room spun. The last thing she wanted to do was throw up, so she snapped her eyes closed until the room stopped moving. "Artemis?"

He stood next to her bed, clean as an ice cube, sparkling and smiling, his heart wide open. He nodded but didn't speak. The unasked question fell between them like a fat toad on its back. Helena turned it over. "What are you doing here?"

He produced a bouquet of daisies and daffodils from behind his back. "Xenia stayed until the doctor promised you'd made it through surgery okay, but she had an emergency at the store that I couldn't help with. I told her I would hang bedside in case you came out of your anesthesia early, at least until Velda or Jasmine or Katrine could arrive, so you awoke to a familiar face."

Helena squeezed her eyes closed then open. She decided that in her new, breastless incarnation, she didn't have the time or patience for confusion. "Are you dating my mother?"

A chuckle started in Artemis' belly, and it rippled along his body until it squeezed through the crinkles in his eyes. When the laughter was gone, he grew as serious as a promise. "Velda and I are friends, always have been, nothing more or less."

He cleared his throat and spoke clearly. "I think you're the most beautiful creature on this earth, and I've never met a stronger heart. Also," he added, "you smell like cinnamon."

Helena peeked at her morphine drip. Was this one of the hallucinations the nurse had warned her about? Was she even awake? She might still be in surgery, under anesthesia. "I'm not up for this conversation right now."

"I understand completely." Artemis eased the flowers into a pitcher of water on the table next to her bed. He pulled a chair out from behind a curtain and then faced it toward the window. "I'll be over here if you need me."

§

It was Velda who proposed the boob funeral and hosted it the same day as Helena's operation. Helena wanted nothing more than to be alone to tend to her body, which felt soft and yellow, like an uncooked yolk. She didn't like all the worried eyes on her. She hated the plummet pace at which everything had happened. She wanted her old life back, her old body.

"I'm fine," she croaked.

"You look tender on the outside," Artemis agreed, "but you're gonna be better than fine. Never doubt that."

If Helena was surprised that Artemis was still here, she didn't show it. Standing next to him were Katrine, then Xenia, Velda, Ursula, and Jasmine. Jasmine hadn't allowed her daughter Tara to attend post-surgery. They all wore black and circled the hospital bed, careful for the drain tubes leaving the area where Helena's breasts had been.

"Did they get it all?" Katrine asked. Helena's beautiful niece, Ursula's daughter, squeezed her hand. Her green Catalain eyes were dusted with concern. She'd returned from London last fall and been in her own bubble since she'd been back. Helena's scare had pulled her back toward the surface.

"I'm sure of it," Xenia said, not giving her sister a chance to respond.

Velda grabbed the hands of the people near her and urged the rest of the circle to do the same. "She's going to be okay. It doesn't take a mindreader to see that," she said, staring at Katrine. "Now, let's focus. We have gathered here to pay our respects to what once was a beautiful pair of knockers."

The group nodded. Tears rolled down Xenia's cheeks.

"Lovely breasts, full like God intended and still riding high after fifty years on the planet." Velda adjusted her hair. "Don't think you ever thanked me for those."

Helena's eyes were closed. She was shaking.

"Is there something you want to say?" Xenia whispered to her sister.

Helena's voice was rough. She knew she was talking to herself, but it felt good to have her family around to reflect it back to her. "Don't say goodbye to me, all right? I've got my fight, and I've got my hips, and I've got my candy. Don't count this old lady out."

"Of course not!" The circle dropped hands and touched her feet and ankles and soft blonde hair, murmuring words of support and love.

"Those surgeons can't touch any part of you that matters, Helena," Artemis said. She believed it was the first time he had spoken her name, and it felt like balm on her skin. "Your spirit is stronger than ever. It's a beautiful thing."

Xenia beamed at the little man who had floated his chair into the sky tied to a bunch of red, blue, and yellow balloons.

"You're not scared," Katrine said in wonder. She smiled the smile of her youth, and it was like the sun rising.

Helena opened her eyes at the warmth of it. "I sure missed that grin. Now who brought me candy?"

"Candy?" Velda asked, shocked. "This isn't a Girl Scout gathering. It's a boob funeral." She pulled out a bottle of brandy. They all were required to take a swallow, but before they did— Velda's rules—they had to share something important that they'd lost.

"Well, I'll go first, you ninnies," Velda said. "I lost my husband. He was a bastard, but I've missed him every single day since then."

"I lost my innocence," Ursula said. Her eyes locked on Velda. She'd barely had time to go home since her emergency return from the Cities.

Xenia was staring at Helena. "I lost my fear."

"I almost lost the woman I love, and it took me fifty-five years to find her," Artemis said. No one questioned him.

"I lost my way," Katrine whispered. She took a swig of the fiery, tawny liquid and handed it to her sister.

"I...lost my balance." Jasmine, Katrine's sister, wet her lips with the brandy and shoved the bottle toward Xenia, who helped Helena to take a sip.

"That's it," Velda said, taking the bottle back and chuckling. "We're a tribe now. A tribe of losers." The words fell like warm rain and drew them all closer.

They stayed for another twenty minutes or so, talking about loss, the weather, and the store. Helena soon drifted off, and they all went home except for Xenia.

§

She was by her sister's side when the young doctor entered the room. "How's she doing?" he asked.

"Sleeping. Do you think you got all the cancer?"

"It's too soon to know for sure, but the prognosis appears excellent. She may even be able to avoid chemotherapy."

Xenia's shoulders relaxed.

"You're sure we still can't talk you into the genetic testing? If we caught it early, we'd have more options."

"No, thank you." Xenia said.

§

Artemis visited Helena every day she was in the hospital. He gave her as much space as she needed but made sure she never felt alone. When she was well enough to sit up, he taught her how to play Bullshit and Euchre with the deck of red Bicycle cards he always carried in his front shirt pocket. He also brought her rich Belgian chocolate and creamy Italian white truffles, books, and news from the store. And every day, he told her how beautiful she was.

It got to where she wondered how she'd ever gotten by without him.

And in the midst of the drama, she *almost* forgot about the papers still in her purse.

The Catalain Book of Secrets:
Accepting Gifts

A gift freely given creates a vacuum. This imbalance moves the recipient to new levels if they accept the gift. A gift accepted with an open heart changes the world.

Always accept the good that is offered to you. Always.

CHAPTER 9

The night after Helena's stitches were removed, she and Xenia walked down to the river behind the Queen Anne. It was a warm spring evening, but it was still March and lacey crusts of ice clung to the river banks. The moon was a slim fingernail in the sky, permitting all the glitter to the stars. The air smelled crisp, like the juice of a green apple.

The twins hadn't planned this. They'd just found themselves at the river bank, where Helena stripped. From behind, her body was curves and cream. The angry red scars on her chest held a hideous beauty. Xenia looked away from them, but not before she witnessed the pain on her sister's face. She refused to glance down at her own body.

"Xenia, do you remember when Velda took us in for professional photographs?"

Velda had driven to Fargo with the girls riding in the back of the station wagon and wearing matching outfits—white dresses, white gloves, and black pillbox hats purchased specifically for this. Ursula had been at school.

"Sula really should be here," Helena had said. She was five.

"Shush," Velda had said. "This is just for twins. I'm going to enter you two in a contest. You'd like that, wouldn't you?"

Xenia raised the logical objection. "But we don't look anything alike."

"That'll make you even more unique." Velda touched up her lipstick in the rearview mirror as she drove. "And we'll stop for chocolate Cokes on the way home."

Helena remembered Xenia being worried. The trip didn't feel right. Her sister started tugging at her black hair like she did when she got nervous.

I don't want to go, Xenia mouthed.

Helena put a finger to her lips in the universal signal for silence. She reached inside her plastic little-girl purse and pulled out a bag of homemade purple marzipan. The texture was a little off, the almond scent a bit too overpowering, but she saw it work as Xenia took a chunk, a soft smile replacing the tight worry on her face as she chewed. She and Helena played rock paper scissors for the rest of the drive, both of them pulling the same gesture each time.

Helena savored the memory, sharing it back and forth with her sister. That's why she was here, naked and shivering on the edge of the river: she needed to soothe her sister, take away her worry, show her that everything would be all right. The stars dropped and sparkled around Helena's body like sweet fireflies.

"I love you at your very center," Xenia said.

Helena shot her a reassuring smile and jumped into the icy water. The cold grabbed her like a slap, stripped away her flesh and wounds and worries, and left that slippery, eternal golden thread that beat with a hot and permanent pulse. She climbed out of the water, trembling but peaceful. She had washed away some fear, enough to get through some more days.

But she didn't tell her sister what she was really thinking. She didn't want to worry her.

Helena was terrified in her deepest heart, and the fear was eroding her from the inside out. She knew it wasn't the cancer that would destroy her. You could excise the tumor and then waste the rest of your life glancing back, mourning what was no longer yours, or worse, looking forward, always wondering when the cancer would return.

Helena was certain that she would never be free again.

The Catalain Book of Secrets: Sisters

Nothing on this earth will double your magic like a sister. If possible, keep one near at all times.

CHAPTER 10

She was healthy enough to move around, and she wore a brave face, but she felt so empty. The trauma of the surgery and the attention of the doctors behind her, she intimately grieved the loss of her breasts. Artemis's company soothed her to a degree, and Xenia was always on the periphery, quick to appear if she needed something, but it wasn't the same as having her body whole. She'd lost part of *herself.*

She'd run the washrag over her chest in the shower. Her front felt like a corrugated, parched stretch of earth, but she refused to look at any part of herself except her face in the mirror. Now that she no longer required a bra, it was easy to avoid glancing down. She wouldn't even watch her feet as she pulled on her socks for fear of catching a glimpse of her flat chest.

The doctor had warned her this could happen. He'd offered her antidepressants. She didn't want medicine. She wanted to be a woman again, curves and jiggles and flesh and warmth.

All the longing for what she was missing exhausted her, to the point that she slept past noon most days, letting Claudette take over for her at Seven Daughters.

She was getting old.

She didn't even care enough about the store or the Queen Anne to worry about Meredith taking them away any more. If Ursula and Xenia found out, they could do something about it. If they didn't find out, didn't everything go wrong in the end anyhow? There was horrible unrest in her family. Her great-niece had disappeared. Something had happened to Katrine. But what did it matter? Nothing was right anymore.

The sense of disquiet was so strong that three days after swimming in the river with Xenia, it drove her outside, into the night.

And onto the backs of the snakes.

She was too empty to even be startled. She simply followed the stream of slipping, hissing, urine-scented reptiles away from the Queen Anne. The crescent moon howled at her. People stared from their windows, horrified by the vision of a broken Helena stumbling across the reptiles, her gray-blonde hair tossed by the sharp breeze. But she didn't stop. She didn't even think.

Across town, she heard a siren.

"Helena Catalain, come inside!"

She glanced over at the woman standing on her porch, her face panicked. Helena shook her head and kept walking. The snakes were inside her head, whispering to her, their melody hypnotizing. They brought images of people she hadn't met and a time she hadn't lived in. The first image was of the Queen Anne in its full, fresh glory, and a woman who looked very much like her niece Katrine walking up the sidewalk wearing an ankle-length brocade dress and a shirtwaist, her hair done in a Gibson Girl.

That image was soon replaced by one of River Street in downtown Faith Falls, which she recognized, though she didn't know the unfamiliar old wooden buildings lining the dirt road or the two white-haired men rocking on a porch. And then the mental pictures whizzed back to a plump man astride a horse constructing a rickety fence on the banks of Rum River, then back further to Indians riding horse across the land that would become Faith Falls, and further, and further.

It was dizzying. She felt like she was walking through time. She would have kept going if the secret snake whispers hadn't abruptly stopped, leaving her both exhausted and energized. She blinked, awaking from the spell.

She stood outside of Meredith Gottfridsen's house. Snakes rubbed over her ankles, slithered across her feet, bumping against and past her, but she could no longer hear their voices, only the cold leather of their bodies rustling against the ground.

And over that, the smallest sound.

She cocked her head. The noise was pure sadness, or was it fear? It seemed to be coming from over her head. She had to squint through the shadows caused by the street lamps to spot the source of the crying: a woman, curled in the lowest branch of the magnificent oak in the rambler's front lawn. She wore a patch over her left eye.

"Meredith?" Helena asked.

The woman hugged her knees tighter to her body, but her weeping didn't stop.

Helena stepped closer, wading through the snakes. It was Meredith, and in addition to the patch, her right eye appeared to be clouding over. "Are you all right?"

"Don't come any closer!" Meredith's voice was ragged. She was staring frantically in every direction, as if she were blind. Groceries were scattered on the ground below her, a gallon of milk here and bag of chips there winking through the thickness of reptiles.

Helena's stomach tumbled. How had Meredith found her way home? She must be nearly blind by now. "Meredith, it's Helena Catalain. The snakes are here. We need to get you inside."

"*You.*" The word was so sharp that the snakes froze for a razor-moment. "You *witch*. You did this to me! And you brought the snakes." Meredith's right shoulder ticked on a rhythm, a clock that counted pain rather than time, and her hands were rubbing circles into the bark of the tree. Left alone with her thoughts and her soul, with her only window into the world clouding by the minute, Meredith was going as crazy as Helena. Crazier, because she hadn't cultivated enough love in her life to survive a low spell.

Helena put her hand on Meredith's ankle, the only part of her she could reach. Meredith flinched. "I'll help you into your house, all right?" Helena asked.

"I'm not letting those snakes touch me." The tic in Meredith's shoulder increased its pace.

Helena's head dropped. She couldn't see her feet for the river of reptiles. They should probably disgust her, but they didn't. "You can ride on my shoulders. Come on now. You can't stay out here all night. You'll be safe inside."

Meredith's mask slipped, but she grabbed it and slapped it back on. "I'll let you help me into the house, *witch*, but that doesn't change anything. I'm still taking your store, and your house."

A puff of anger ignited in Helena. For a moment, she considered walking away. Meredith had created her own pain, on the whole, and she had nursed it like a beloved child. If Meredith hadn't looked so lonely, so absolutely lost, things may have ended differently.

As it was, like every woman since the beginning of time, Helena moved her own pain to the side to make room to help someone else carry theirs.

There was work to be done.

The Catalain Book of Secrets: Equinox Spell

The vernal equinox has always been symbolic of new life. Also, because day and night are of equal length on the equinox, it is a time of balance and harmony. It is the best time to set things to right and to plant the seeds that you want to grow in the new year. This simple ritual will ensure your safety, prosperity, and joy:

Materials:

1 egg
1 purple scarf
Paint (egg paint, if you can find it, or tempera paint; you'll need lots of red)
Pine needles and sage
Paper and pen

Instructions:

1. Three days before the vernal equinox, set the pine needles and sage in a small bowl in your workspace. Start them smoldering. With the bowl in your hand, face each of the four directions, centering yourself in your heart and spirit.

2. Once you've cleansed your space and yourself, place the bowl near you. Ensure that it keeps smoldering.

3. Write down your hopes for the new year on the paper, then fold it until it is a strip about an inch wide.

4. Paint the egg, thinking about your hopes for the new year as you do. The more red you use, the more powerful your hopes will be, but don't make the mistake of using only red. Contrast magnifies.

5. Let the egg dry.

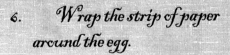

6.   Wrap the strip of paper
       around the egg.

7. Wrap the egg in the purple scarf.
    Put it under your pillow, and
    sleep on it for two nights.

8.   On the third night, the night of
      the equinox, retrieve the scarf from
      under your pillow. Unwrap it and
      remove the paper and the egg.

9.   Burn the paper to release your dreams
     into the Universe.

10. If weather permits, go outside with the
     egg and crack it onto the ground to set
     the wheel of infinite possibilities into
     motion.

11. Be grateful.

CHAPTER 11

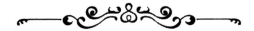

"You sure you want to go through with it this year?"

Helena nodded. The worry was spelled across Xenia's face. It had replaced the surprise that had exploded when Helena told her what she meant to do. After all, there had been so many crises in their family lately, and such a big cleansing on the night the snakes had run like water through the streets of Faith Falls.

"I'm sure," Helena said.

Helena and Xenia cleared the Queen Anne's drawing room except for a ring of chairs that hugged the walls. From year to year, they never knew how many would show up for the equinox celebration. No invitations were ever sent.

Food was prepared—morsels of smoked rabbit nestled in a creamy potato broth, lavender-infused Duck L'orange covered in crispy, sweet-salty skin, tiny quails stuffed with sage dressing, wild perch drizzled with onion jam, roasted garlic soup with poached eggs, haricot verts in a lemon-almond sauce, roasted butternut squash, delicate mushroom caps filled with salty bacon, wild rice, and poached raisins, fresh spinach dressed with poppyseed vinaigrette, a wild lettuce salad speckled with sunflower nuts and bits of bright, fresh orange, platters of grapes, apples, nuts, and cheeses, pomegranates seeds piled high like a tower of glistening rubies, blood orange slices as gorgeous as a rising sun, fresh-baked bread still steaming and scenting the air with the smell of home and hearth.

For dessert, Helena and Claudette had prepared fresh strawberries with lemon verbena pudding, crystallized rose petals, wild angelica meringues, cherry, apple, and banana cream pies, quarter-sized violet and hazelnut cakes, and rich chocolate candies with fluted edges and curving lips. They'd also mulled cider thick with cloves and the sharp mystery of cinnamon and arranged the chairs, but that's all they could do.

The house could feel their excitement beating deep in their hearts with a scarlet heat. The vernal equinox was the time of all possibilities, the day and then night when the year of struggle and pain could be laid down without guilt or worry, and the forthcoming year of hope and light could be welcomed. There had been much necessary pain recently, so much so that the air had grown warped from it.

"How many clients did Ursula meet with this year?" Xenia asked.

Helena shrugged and arranged her chocolates for the seventh time. "I remember seeing twenty or so, but I think one might have been the new mailman going to the wrong door. I wish she'd tell us, so we'd know how much food to prepare."

As far as they knew, there wasn't an exact correlation between Ursula's clients and the number of people who showed up at the celebration, but there did seem to be a connection. It was as if Ursula's magic needed the final seal of the equinox to become permanent. Her clients, at least the most aware ones, sensed this and were drawn like fireflies to the Queen Anne on March 19, 20, or 21 of every year, depending on which day the vernal equinox fell.

But they weren't the only ones who felt compelled to approach the house, knock hesitantly on the magnificent scrolled front door, stand outside shifting from foot to foot, entering apologetically once the door was opened. They'd claim not to know why they'd come, and were surprised when they were welcomed.

Helena expected a record turnout of attendees this year since the weather was glorious. The lilacs, tired of quivering with unspent beauty, burst open, sending purple honey into the air six weeks earlier than ever recorded. Bluebirds warbled, cocking their heads at the sleepy worms that peeked out to wonder where the snow had gone. The high of the day had been 72 degrees, breaking all sorts of records.

The house waited. Inside, Ursula laughed spontaneously and often, finding reasons to smile in every room. Xenia had already poured herself a glass of Chianti. Helena bustled. Katrine watched the door.

The first knock sent ichor through each of their veins, steadying them.

The equinox celebration had begun.

Helena answered the knock. "Leo!" She wrapped him in a hug. "I'm so happy you're here. Please, come in."

After him strolled a woman who smelled like an ocean, then Xenia's Cleo, followed by the local second grade teacher, her expression so nervous that her eyes spun like a deer's, followed by Artemis who carried a bonsai tree as a hostess gift, then Velda, then a woman who called herself Merry but who didn't let her smile travel past her face. And they just kept coming, eating and talking and wondering.

A fire blazed in the marble fireplace, cozying the gigantic room. An open window on the opposite wall kept the space from growing stuffy, the brisk, warming air dancing with the smell of woodsmoke. Some of the guests had entered through the back door. They were talking to people they'd never met inside a house most of them had never visited. If someone had pulled the shades and turned off the lights, they would have witnessed the sparks of electricity passing between each guest.

A bottle of champagne was opened, and then another. Cheeks grew rosy, and the connections multiplied to the point that cartoon-perfect lightning bolts could be observed shooting between people. Helena brought out eggs to be painted, and the visitors fell to work decorating them before hiding them around the house, bumping into one another and giggling.

At one point, Artemis asked Claudette if it was okay if he touched her.

"Sure," she said. There were only a few empty spots on her, on the tips of her fingertips, under her hair.

Artemis reached out and gently brushed her shoulder. She clenched, but no tattoo appeared. He nodded as if he'd expected this, and from across the room, Helena beamed at him.

Two women and a man who had entered through the back door talked about the weather and glanced at their watches. They didn't have any place they needed to be, but time felt like the only real thing in the room. Leo kept the buffet looking nice, rearranging poppy cakes and spring flowers glazed with sugar to fill in spots and wiping off crumbs.

And then, as if they had always been there, Jasmine and Tara arrived, and everyone found their seats. All the guests sat in a circle in the drawing room, the buffet tables behind them, a large empty space in the middle. If they had drinks or plates balanced with food, they placed them at their feet. A few of them shuffled uncomfortably, looking from face to face for a clue of what was expected of them. The town had blown the top off of many of its secrets the night the snakes had emerged, but Helena could tell by looking at Claudette that there were many more below. That sort of thing is always a process.

But before the second level of secrets could be reached, Helena had a surprise for them all, and it arrived just on time.

"I've got it," Helena said in response to the doorbell. She hoped the fear wasn't apparent in her voice.

Chapter 12

"Greetings, Meredith!"

'Greetings' was an odd word for Helena to use. She was nervous. She hadn't seen Meredith since the night she'd perched her on her shoulders and teetered into her home. She'd helped Meredith to her living room, averting her eyes as they passed Michael Baum's sleeping form on the couch, the smell of alcohol rolling off of him in visible waves. At Meredith's request, she'd gotten her a glass of water, and then she'd left and never spoken to anyone of the incident, also at Meredith's request.

She stepped aside to allow Meredith and her two guests to enter. She recognized Burt Winters, who sat on the city council. Helena guessed that the other woman, her back so stiff she could have balanced a book on her head, was an attorney.

Meredith shuffled in, her arm hooked inside Burt's, her free hand extended in front of her to feel the air. It pained Helena to see Meredith's dark sunglasses. She imagined the woman must be entirely blind in the one eye and only able to sense light or dark in the other.

Yet, she maintained an attitude of arrogance, somehow. An arching eyebrow appeared over the top of her dark glasses. The equinox party was out of sight, but the breath and soul of forty people in the house was unmistakable. "Having a get-together?"

Helena's knees knocked. Today was thirty days after Meredith had first delivered the papers. She was here to take the house away, and the store. Helena had, in fact, invited her over the phone just yesterday. She hadn't told Xenia or Ursula or anyone. She also hadn't thought this plan through thoroughly. "Yes. Care to join us?"

Meredith's head drew back, and she barked an incredulous laugh in the direction of Burt and her female companion. There would be no quarter given for the fact that Helena had helped her out of the tree, her knees clamped around Helena's neck. If anything, her shame at someone seeing her husband passed out drunk and the fact that she had had to accept help worked like gasoline on her fire. "Don't pretend you don't know why we're here. Vicky, deliver the papers."

The house cracked with the sound of ice snapping. The attorney glanced up, startled.

"Spring thaw," Meredith said. "Give her the papers."

Vicky set her briefcase on the entry table and popped it open. Ursula strode into the foyer, followed by Xenia, both coming to check on what was taking Helena so long.

"What the hell?" Xenia asked. "You have a fine nerve coming here."

Ursula's eyes glittered. She was built sturdy, like Helena, but lacked her softness. "All are welcome. Even Meredith Gottfridsen." She indicated the drawing room.

Xenia's mouth grew tight. "I don't think she can see what's right in front of her eyes. Can you, Meredith?"

It was a cruel question. Meredith began to shake with fury, the smell of sulfur and heat leaving her in waves.

"Please," Helena said, reaching for the tray of equinox candies that she'd been saving for this exact moment. They were shaped like diary keys, each no larger than a thumbnail. It was early to serve them, but this might be the only chance she had. "Take one."

She thrust a candy into Meredith's hand. The woman stroked the smooth milk chocolate with her thumb. A tear rolled from under her glasses, a single water drop tinted pink with blood.

"What is it?" she whispered. She sounded suspicious. Helena believed she had every right to be.

"I made it for you."

It may have been the clear blue truth of Helena's words, or the power of the house, or Meredith's blindness giving her the power to smell the cure for her loneliness.

Or maybe she was just hungry.

Whatever it was, she placed the chocolate in her mouth.

She chewed vigorously, brown foaming the edges of her lips.

She swallowed, the ball of chocolate sliding down her snake throat.

Her head fell forward and her glasses followed, sliding off her nose and onto the floor. Her eyes were horrible, wicked yellow crust rimmed with red sealing all but the edge of one.

"In middle school, I was called horse face." Meredith covered her mouth as if she had just burped in public. The eye that was not entirely sealed widened a hair. "Get it? 'Mare-edith?'"

"Are you all right?" Burt asked, ignoring her words, horrified by her face. "Your eyes."

Helena held the key tray toward him. He grabbed a candy with something like desperation. Vicky followed suit.

"Come in," Helena offered tenderly. "Please. All the way, I mean." She pushed Ursula and Xenia toward the drawing room, hoping the three in the foyer would follow them, knowing there was nothing more she could do if they didn't. She passed around the tray of key candies to the seated guests, her eyes traveling toward the drawing room door, her hands shaking.

Burt, Vicky, and Meredith didn't follow.

The Catalains were going to lose this house, and the store. Her candies must not have been strong enough.

The equinox candy keys were her most secret recipe, concocted of the rarest cacao, candied prunes, the essence of rose petals, and the lightest dusting of moonflower pollen. They tasted of royal jelly, the color purple, and a sweetness so pure that it made a popping sound when swallowed. The noise signaled a deep and deliciously painful healing in the cracked land between hearts and mouths.

Tears flowed freely down Helena's cheeks. She had tried, in the best way she knew how, to help Meredith. It hadn't worked, and she was going to lose everything. She should have asked for help so much earlier, but she hadn't, and so here she was. All she could do was heal those in front of her. She continued to pass around the chocolate keys.

Then, quietly, Meredith walked in, Burt and Vicky immediately behind her.

Helena cried out in relief. "Please, I've saved you chairs."

Burt and Vicky glanced in awe around the drawing room but followed her without protest, leading Meredith. Helena believed the thumping of her heart could be heard all the way over in Alexandria.

The fire was crackling. When Xenia spoke, an explosion of wood sent a glowing orange spark to her feet. She stomped it out without glancing down, saving an angry stare for Meredith. Still, she spoke. She couldn't help it. She'd eaten one of the chocolate keys. "I'm afraid Helena will die before me."

The warm tears bubbling up in Helena's eyes doubled, and she set her tray down and rushed over to Xenia, grabbing her hand. "I'm afraid of that, too. Who will take care of you?"

And so it began, the releasing of secrets.

Leonardo nodded. "I'm worried that none of you will see me, and if you do, that I won't measure up." He glanced down at his feet. "And I'm worried that if I do measure up, I'll never be able to let down my guard, because you'll always expect that much of me."

Cleo shook her head, and her jewels and metal rings jangled like fairy bells. She glanced over at Xenia. "I took one of Ursula's spells. I think that's the only reason I met you."

"What?" Xenia asked. Helena couldn't tell if she was going to laugh or cry.

Cleo glanced down at her hands. "Ursula gave me a tiny ruby-colored glass bottle the week before I came into Seven Daughters. She told me to warm it with my body and then drink it. I held it in my hand and found myself across from the store. I drank it. It tasted like crushed aspirin and ear wax. I started coughing, and so I went into Seven Daughters for water. And I'm afraid to be a lesbian," Cleo continued. "But I am." Her chair rose a hair's breadth off the ground.

With every secret told, a tattoo faded from Claudette's flesh. First the cross went from her cheek, and then the horrible ferret demon began to erase itself from her neck. She sat taller.

Seeing this, the second grade teacher cleared her throat. "I'm…um, I'm grateful you invited me to this party." Her eyes raced around the circle, almost hopeful someone would contradict her. "I think, if I'm reading this right, that the hostess gift is to tell a story? Well, I don't remember this well, but I want to share the story of Hewitt. It's one of the very few things I keep my mouth shut about. People I work with will tell you I'm a talker," she added, a sad smile introducing her face.

"Hewitt was my 5th grade classmate and the poorest kid in our class. We always teased him about smelling like manure. You know how kids are. That winter was really snowy, and when the temperature dropped below zero, our teachers had us spend recesses in the classroom. One of these frigid days, all three of the 5th grade teachers were together a room or two over, leaving us alone for… how long I'm not sure. What I remember is that by the time they returned to the classroom, we'd strung up Hewitt by his neck and were hanging him using the door as a fulcrum." She gasped, as if she was listening to someone else tell the story. Her eyes had locked on Ursula's, whose gaze didn't waver.

"Hewitt was trying to get a grip on the rope around his neck, his feet scraping at the air. He hung up there like a trussed pig, with two kids on the other side of the door holding the end of the rope. His hand-me-down shoes were inches from the floor. I think what alerted the teachers was the class chant. Simple, loud. *Hang Hewitt.* The first word was longer than the second. *Haaaaaang Hewitt ... haaaaaang Hewitt.*"

She coughed. She glanced at her trembling hands, then back at Helena, her voice tight. "I don't know if I was chanting too, or if I was silent, but that's not why I've never told this story to anyone. I don't tell it because I don't know whether we never saw Hewitt again or if he was back the next day."

The man next to her, whom she'd never met before she'd entered the house, patted her shoulder. Tears were running down Claudette and Helena's faces and seeing that, the second grade teacher began to cry as well. Her tears smelled like sage.

A man who had entered through the back door recognized himself in that secret. "No one knows who I really am. I don't let them." He appeared apologetic. The air around him turned red, then faded to peach.

"Me neither," Meredith whispered. And then she jumped up, knocking her chair over. "Me neither!"

The Queen Anne sent its thanks to the moon.

The Catalain Book of Secrets:
Celebration with Strangers

Certain alchemy needs to happen in
the company of others. The flame of
communion can burn away even the
deepest of suffering. Reach out, and
you will be rewarded.

CHAPTER 13

A month after the equinox party, Xenia stepped tentatively across the threshold of Immanuel Lutheran Church.

"You won't really burst into flames," Helena said. "That'd be ridiculous."

The music inside was glorious, a chorus of angels with a single, gritty thread running through it that made the rest of the voices even more pure by contrast. Still, Xenia's discomfort was palpable.

Helena grabbed her sister's elbow and pointed with her chin. Ninety percent of the women inside the church were wearing a Xenia dress. The woman in the pew nearest them wore a lemon-yellow sleeveless poplin sundress with a red sash that Xenia had sewn two summers ago. It was brilliant, crisp, and the woman wearing it shone brightly. Next to her was a lady wearing another of Xenia's creations, this one a cap-sleeved, 40s-style cotton dress with tiny white polka dots on blue cotton. Its cut accented her tiny waist and large hips and imparted on her an overall aura of capability. The whole church was lit up by women looking their best and feeling their strongest in Xenia's dresses.

A grateful smile flooded Xenia's face.

But the most amazing creation of all was worn by Cleo, who stood in the front of the congregation, lead soprano in the choir. She looked like an exquisite ocean queen in her muslin dress hand-dyed so ingeniously by Xenia that undulating blue ran into shades of green to create the effect of flowing water across Cleo's flat stomach and round hips.

The dress was both modest in its coverage and powerful in what it implied by revealing the strength of her forearms, the intelligence of her hands, the quickness of her ankles. She didn't move as she sang, but such was the power of the dress that it made her shimmer like she was the music itself, her beautiful tiger eyes closed, her thick jungle hair falling off her shoulders. The music that rippled out of her mouth matched her glory. Her voice was pure crystal that entered behind one's heart.

Xenia was spellbound looking at her, as was much of the congregation. Helena tapped her lightly on the shoulder and pointed toward the usher.

"Welcome," he said. "Would you like to sit up front? We have a seat near the choir saved especially for you." He was a young man whose smile seemed far older than him. "You too," he said, smiling at Helena.

Helena was grateful for the guidance and followed her sister toward the front of the church, taking the last seat in the wooden pew directly across from the choir. At this vantage point, she was able to identify another person in the choir.

Meredith.

The two women nodded at each other, Meredith's eyes bright and clear but her mouth still tight. Helena was okay with that. She knew these sorts of things were a process. At least Meredith had shut down the eminent domain process and stopped picketing the store.

For now.

The entire sermon was beautiful, about love and hope and learning from mistakes. That night, Xenia finally made love to Cleo, or more accurately, they finally made love to each other. Xenia was hiding secret folds under flowing clothes, and she took Cleo into them, loving the warm, wet musk of her body, the firmness of her breasts. She had an acute sensation of wanting to be everything to Cleo, simultaneously embracing her and inside of her. Cleo was as flexible as a ribbon, her mouth warm and yielding. They twined in the bedsheets until dawn, bringing each other again and again to exquisite heights of ecstasy, and finally fell into a dreamless sleep, cozy in each other's arms, their glorious dresses pooled on the floor where they'd first tossed them.

Helena awoke the next morning with the glow of her twin's experience. Her heart danced with the joy of it. Xenia was in love, and the commitment was being returned to her in full.

Helena was quiet as she got ready for work in the rumpled dawn light. The store wouldn't open for three hours, but she'd agreed to meet Claudette early to work on a new chocolate recipe.

She knew Claudette was trying to drag her back to her former self. Though she still refused to peek below her neck, the equinox party had helped her to make peace with the fact that she could never celebrate her body again. That felt something like healing, enough to let her look for joy elsewhere. A consistent delight was found in mentoring Claudette.

Claudette had the gift, and she'd brought a younger flair to the Seven Daughters sweets, introducing transparent, cinnamon-flavored hard candies that changed color in your mouth depending on your mood and licorice bracelets and rings ingeniously designed to look like authentic jewelry and deliver a treat in a pinch. Helena's classics were still the bestsellers, but customers were sampling Claudette's creations and coming back for seconds.

Her mirror candies were a crowd favorite. No longer than her pinky and poured into an elegant mold she'd created herself, the dark chocolates were shaped like old-fashioned hand mirrors with a sugar-glass reflection. She dusted them with crystallized ginger and specks of rock salt. The ginger bits were at first hard in your mouth, but as the chocolate melted, the ginger blended with the salt, which then popped before melting into your tongue. Eating them imbued the person with the courage to face themselves.

Claudette had told Helena that she'd discovered the power of her new candy the day after the equinox party, when she'd sampled her first mirror out of the tray, not even waiting until it cooled. It tasted so incredible—the perfect mixture of sweet and salty, crunchy and creamy—that she ate the whole batch. Rather than getting a stomachache, she was overcome with an abundance of unwanted clarity. She'd realized she'd been hiding in her own flesh, adding on layers so she would never face the world unprotected.

With the awareness the candy mirrors brought her, she changed her eating habits, though not dramatically. There was too much good food in the world, and too much pleasure in enjoying it. She altered her patterns just enough so that she began to feel comfortable in herself. Then, she began to claim her own body. Once she did that, there was no looking back. She started walking to work and soon, she no longer grew short of breath on busy days or when she mounted a flight of stairs.

The post-mirror-candy Claudette was only 15 pounds lighter than the previous version, and she discovered she loved herself at that weight. And she wanted to pass that gift onto Helena, whose post-mastectomy depression was written in the slump of her shoulders and the dullness of her eyes. Yet, Helena refused to eat a mirror.

Claudette might have let it go at that if not for one batch of chocolates that Helena had crafted yesterday. They were plain truffles, shaped like tiny eggs. Not knowing that Helena had meant to toss them in the garbage and bury them under paper, Claudette had popped one in her mouth. The sense of loss was immediate, powerful, the pain in her chest almost unbearable, like she was being sliced in two. Claudette spit out the candy, scouring at her mouth to remove any trace of it, gasping for breath. She began crying for reasons she couldn't explain. Claudette realized what she had eaten: unfinished, bodiless breasts.

Once she'd tasted Helena's pain, nothing could stop her from healing it. She had spent the entire evening in the store, just finishing her task as Helena unlocked the front door on this warm spring morning and made her way into the kitchen.

"You beat me here!" Helena said, an honest smile on her face. "Well, let's get to it. Should we start with the caramel apple truffle we were talking about?"

Claudette shook her head and held out the brown box she'd barely had time to tie a ribbon on. She hurried to her car and took off before Helena could respond, let alone open the gift. Curious, Helena loosened the pink ribbon and slid the top off the box.

She gulped.

Inside was the most elegant creation she'd ever seen. Claudette was a skilled engineer, but this candy surpassed anything Helena could even imagine.

The box held an intricate candy tree whose trunk was the size of Helena's thumb. The bark was three different kinds of chocolate blended together in a seamless natural pattern capturing the shades of brown. The roots of the tree were also chocolate but curved around a glowing red heart crafted of rock candy so delicate it looked like blown glass.

Rather than leaves, the trees branches were covered with vibrant butterflies each the size of a freckle. Helena touched her tongue to one of them, a blue creature with swirls of white and green accenting its snowflake sugar candy wings. The tiniest taste made her heart soar. Her smile turned into laughter, and she tipped her face to the sun in gratitude.

Although some would have considered it too lovely to eat, Helena knew good medicine when she saw it and had devoured the candy on her drive to Artemis' house, starting with the sweet crunch of the butterflies and working her way down the white, milk, and dark chocolate branches and trunk. When she pulled into his driveway, all that remained was the rose-flavored rock candy heart melting sweetly on her tongue.

She found him drinking coffee on his porch, as she'd hoped he would be. He set down his crossword puzzle and stood, his mouth tight with concern. His eyes, though, were open and safe, their edges wrinkled from years of laughter and adventure. He smelled of shaving cream, and his shirt was ironed despite the early hour.

"Come with me, please." She took his hand, and his face softened immediately. She led him to his bedroom. She sat him on his queen-sized bed. The golden-orange of the rising sun warmed the corners of the room, falling gently on the bed with its white quilt, the simple dresser and vanity, both a dark maple and handmade, the bookshelf.

Across the room stood a full-length mirror much like the one she'd danced in front of a million nights ago. For a moment, she lost her courage. She hadn't looked at her body since the surgery. Below her neck, she believed, she was deformed, a dissected woman. But the rock candy heart beat inside of her, and the strength of the dark chocolate roots grounded, and her transformation maybe, just maybe wasn't the terror she'd imagined.

Quickly, she unbuttoned her blouse, standing in front of the mirror. Below it she wore only a camisole. She pulled that over her head. Her eyes snapped shut.

She couldn't do it.

She couldn't look.

She heard the bed creak. Artemis stood behind her. He placed his warm steady hands on her shoulders. "Look," he said. The word reverberated, and its echo gave her the last bit of nerve she needed.

She opened one eye. Then the other. Her front was flat.

First, it appeared alien and slashed, but she leaned closer to the mirror. It couldn't be! Not believing the reflection, she was forced to glance down at her own flesh. Her eyes hadn't deceived her.

The scars weren't cruel slashes.

They were vines crisscrossing her heart, the edges of the scar tissue unfurled like delicate pink leaves, creating a garden across her chest.

She covered her mouth in amazement. She turned and pulled Artemis into her arms, hugging him all the way to her skin, closer to her heart than she'd ever hugged anyone before.

She was finally ready to start causing trouble in this world.

Oh yes she was, and it would be the best kind.

ACKNOWLEDGMENTS

I love the Catalains, and their gorgeous Queen Anne, and the quirky town of Faith Falls. This novella is me being unable to let go of them, and specifically, me wanting to find out more about Helena, who was so quiet in The Catalain Book of Secrets. She reminds me a bit of my grandma, Bernie, who I miss on a regular basis. I hope you enjoyed hanging out with her as much as I did.

So many people make it possible for me to craft these stories, but there are three standouts who I want to thank here. First, my mom, who not only watches my kids one day a week so I don't have to stop writing at the end of the day, who not only has encouraged my love of words since I demanded everyone call me "Cursive" at age five, but who also reads the first draft of everything I write, encourages me through the early limping stages, and then copy edits (on super short notice, usually) all my books before they go to print. If you see any errors, it's her fault.

The second person I need to thank is Tony. He is responsible for the gorgeous family tree in all the Catalain books, as well as the layout of the Book of Secrets pages, and much of the ideas that went into the front covers of the books. His creativity and his consistent, unwavering support of my dreams take my writing and joy to new levels. I am thankful every day he's in my life.

Finally, I want to thank Linda Joffe Hull, the woman to whom I dedicated this novella. She supported The Catalain Book of Secrets at a crucial time. The manuscript had gotten oh-so-close to being picked up by three different publishing houses, but ultimately was turned down by all three. Linda offered to edit the manuscript, even though she was behind deadline herself, and she gave me wonderful feedback, including the infamous, "this book has heart, and now it needs a spine." Those words, and the direction to implement them, made me see all the possibilities in the Catalains, and I hope will continue to inspire me to keep visiting Faith Falls.

Thank you.

The Catalain Book of Secrets series is Jessica Lourey's first venture into magical realism, a genre she's loved since she was a teenager. She's best known for her critically-acclaimed Murder-by-Month mysteries, which have earned multiple starred reviews from *Library Journal* and *Booklist,* the latter writing, "It's not easy to make people laugh while they're on the edge of their seats, but Lourey pulls it off...[A] very clever series." Jessica is a tenured professor of creative writing and sociology at a Minnesota college. When not teaching, reading, traveling, writing, or raising her two wonderful kids, you can find her dreaming of her next story. If you enjoyed *Seven Daughters: A Catalain Book of Secrets* novella, please check out *The Catalain Book of Secrets.* You can find out more about Jessica and her books at www.jessicalourey.com.

CPSIA information can be obtained at www.ICGtesting.com
Printed in the USA
LVOW11s1910020615

440866LV00006B/810/P

9 780990 834281